You'll Like It Here
(Everybody Does)

You'll Like It Here
(Everybody Does)

RUTH WHITE

DELACORTE PRESS

Text copyright © 2011 by Ruth White
Jacket art copyright © 2011 by Zdenko Basic

All rights reserved. Published in the United States by Delacorte Press, an imprint of Random House Children's Books, a division of Random House, Inc., New York.

Delacorte Press is a registered trademark and the colophon is a trademark of Random House, Inc.

Grateful acknowledgment is made to Memory Lane Music Group for permission to reprint lyrics from "The Lion Sleeps Tonight," written by George David Weiss, Luigi Creatore, Hugo Peretti & Solomon Linda, copyright © 1961, copyright renewed 1989 and assigned to Abilene Music LLC c/o Larry Spier Music LLC. All rights reserved. International copyright secured. Reprinted by permission of Memory Lane Music Group.

Visit us on the Web! www.randomhouse.com/kids
Educators and librarians, for a variety of teaching tools, visit us at www.randomhouse.com/teachers

Library of Congress Cataloging-in-Publication Data
White, Ruth.
    You'll like it here (everybody does) / Ruth White. — 1st ed.
       p. cm.
    Summary: Although Meggie Blue seems to be an average sixth-grader she is abnormally frightened when residents of her small, North Carolina town become fixated on aliens and soon she and her family are forced to flee, making it clear that all is not as it seems.
    ISBN 978-0-385-73998-6 (hc : alk. paper) —ISBN 978-0-385-90813-9 (glb : alk. paper) – ISBN 978-0-375-89860-0 (ebook) [1. Extraterrestrial beings—Fiction. 2. Family life—Fiction. 3. Interplanetary travel—Fiction. 4. Science fiction.] I Title. II. Title: You will like it here (everybody does).
    PZ7.W58446You 2011
    [Fic]—dc22
                                                    2010032153

The text of this book is set in 12¼-point Goudy.
Book design by Vikki Sheatsley
Printed in the United States of America
10 9 8 7 6 5 4 3 2
First Edition

To: Bill, Kathy, and Anna

You'll Like It Here
(Everybody Does)

· 1 ·

Meggie Speaks

When I was in the third grade on the California coast, a crazy man came into my classroom one day and started waving a knife around. He said he was an alien hunter. He had a purple blotch on his face that was shaped exactly like Mexico, and his eyes were wild. Help came before he could hurt anybody, but he left scars all the same.

I was so petrified I don't remember a thing after that, until I saw Gramps holding out his arms to me. He lifted me from the couch in the principal's office, where I lay curled up, and held me close. He smelled like freshly baked bread.

And that was the day my nightmares started.

At the end of that school term, Mom quit her job at the university, where she taught astronomy, and found a new one at another university, in North Carolina. A moving van carried our belongings across the country, but Mom, Gramps, my brother, David, and I spent five amazing days and nights traveling in our car, taking in the sights of America.

In North Carolina we were thrilled to pieces with our own seven-acre plot of land surrounding the farmhouse Mom had bought for us. Locally it was called the old Fischer place, for the family who'd lived there for years and years before us. There were apple trees and lots of blackberry bushes, a grape arbor, a weeping cherry tree, and I don't know what all.

I barely remember Daddy, who died when I was three. From then on, Gramps, who is my mom's father, tended our house and took care of us. David and I never knew Grandmama, because she died before we were even old enough to have a memory. Gramps, in his sixties, was still as energetic and feisty as a boy. He took good care of himself through a healthy diet and exercise, and because of that, he seemed much younger than he was. At times, in fact, when asked his age, he actually fibbed, subtracting five years or so, and he got away with it.

My mother was the best mom in the world. She was strong like a rock, sweet, smart, and pretty too, but it was Gramps I turned to when I needed help or comfort or affection, probably because he was always available. Gramps was also a wannabe artist. In California he stayed at home and happily painted his pictures when Mom, David, and I were at school. Sometimes he sold his stuff at arts festivals for a few dollars each. But now that we were older, and living in a new place, he wanted to walk out into the world a bit, as he put it. So that first September he began teaching art to high school students in the small town near us. Next door to the high school were the lower schools, where David and I enrolled. Mom's new job was only thirty minutes away. So there we were, a happy bunch of campers in our new home.

The next spring we sowed our seeds in the ground and watched them sprout and grow into living plants that made tomatoes and cucumbers for us, along with green peppers, corn, and melons. We got good vibes from the earth and spent every hour possible outside. Another planting season flew by, and now it's spring again. David and I are practically all grown up, as I am finishing the sixth grade and he the eighth.

The nightmares that started for me in the third grade eased up over the years, but at certain times I still feel like that little girl who was so scared and helpless, she wet her pants. I see things in the shadows, and when I round a corner, I halfway expect something hideous to jump out at me. I also hear noises under my bed and in my closet.

Some shrink told Mom that it's common for a person to carry a thing like this forever. That doesn't exactly make me feel any better. It doesn't help either having a brother who is perfect—one who works out complicated math problems just for the fun of it, and beats the computer in chess. Yeah, David's so middle-aged he makes me sick, and do you think he's ever been afraid of anything at all? I don't think so.

I've come to the conclusion that I'm sure about only one thing in my life, and that is that I want to be able to do something—anything—that my brother can't do. At least, I want to do it *better* than he does. Will that ever happen?

Now at school a new buzz has started. You know the way things go around. One year you'll have stories about witchcraft, and who might be a witch and who might be a vampire or a werewolf. One year there's a ghost in somebody's house, or at one of the umpteen cemeteries in our little town. Everybody has a hair-raising story to tell you at lunch break. And this year, wouldn't you know? It's UFOs.

"There are aliens among us," the kids whisper, because teachers don't want to hear junk like that.

"They are here to take over the earth."

"If we don't get them first, they'll get us."

My very best friend is Kitty—short for Kathryn—Singer, a tiny, sparkly African American girl who always wears purple. I love her to pieces, but I gotta tell you she has an imagination that won't quit. Maybe it's because both her parents are librarians, and the whole family reads tons of stories, sci-fi and otherwise. They also watch every movie that comes along, no matter how far-out.

On a golden Saturday in May, Kitty and I are picking strawberries from our patch when she says to me, "Did you know the aliens come in the middle of the night when you're sleeping, and suck your soul out through your big toe? Then you become one of them, and you don't even know it. You go on living regular until one day they make you do evil things."

"Suck out your soul through your big toe? Kitty, you've been watching way too much sci-fi."

She stands up and wipes her hands on her purple shirt. "Meggie B., I'm serious as a heart attack!" she says. "And when you wake up some night with one of them tugging at your foot, don't come crying to me! I warned you."

Then we both bust out laughing. Kitty always makes me laugh. We whisper secrets and share dreams. We like the same music. We both like Taylor Swift better than Miley Cyrus. We love pretty clothes. Kitty's slogan for life is "All good things start with a dream." We've been working on a slogan for me, but nothing seems to fit yet.

That same afternoon, as we sit in the grass and eat our strawberries, she tells me she likes Corey Marshall, who's in our class.

"I like him too," I say, not getting her drift.

"No," she says, "I mean I don't just like him. I *like*, like him."

"Oh," I say. "You *like* him?"

"Yeah, and if you ever tell a living soul, I will put a curse on you. I do voodoo."

"You do?"

"Who do?" she squeals.

"You do voodoo?" says me.

"Voodoo doo-doo," she comes back.

This could go on all day, so I get to the subject at hand. "Corey Marshall, huh?"

She claps a hand over my mouth, and I mumble through her fingers, "I won't tell."

"There's nothing to tell," she says, and removes her hand.

"That's exactly right. There's nothing to tell. But . . ." I lean over and whisper in her ear. "He sure is cute."

She grins.

I know Kitty and my other classmates don't even believe their own stories about the aliens, but those creepy dreams start crawling around in my head like they used to. In my sleep I see the man with that purple Mexico on his face. I hear him growling, *"I'm an alien hunter. I'm an alien hunter."* And once again his words echo . . . echo . . . echo . . . through my nights and sometimes through my days.

From the first of May until the last of September, Mom, Gramps, David, and I like to sleep on cots on our screened upstairs porch under the stars. I really love those nights. The radio plays low while Mom points out the constellations to us, and I drift off to sleep with the sound of music and Mom's sweet voice.

"There's the Southern Crown."

In the jungle, the mighty jungle

"There's Ursa Minor."

The lion sleeps tonight.

"There's Lupus, the wolf."

Near the village, the peaceful village

"There's Sagittarius, the archer."

The lion sleeps tonight.

Sometimes I wake up in the wee hours to see Mom standing still with her hands on the screen, looking up at the sky. Tears glisten in her blue eyes. Her lips are moving like she's speaking to God, but she doesn't say anything. My mom is so pretty with the moonlight shining on her pale hair. I know at these moments, without being told, that she's thinking of Dad, and is searching for him in the stars.

At school the rumors become more grotesque and bloody with each telling. In my nightmares, yucky creatures climb up the outside wall of our house and onto the porch where we lie sleeping. They have the wild eyes of the madman, and they carry knives.

Other times I wake up crying. David groans and throws a pillow over his head, but Mom holds me while Gramps says comforting things.

"There's nobody out there," he says. "Nobody's going to get our Meggie. We're here to take care of you."

Hush, my darling, don't fear, my darling
The lion sleeps tonight.

Then I go to sleep again under the stars that shine over the North Carolina countryside, far away from the shores of California, where a madman wanted to hurt me.

· 2 ·

On the last day of school, Mom, Gramps, David, and I sit around the table in our shabby-chic kitchen.

"Where do we want to go this summer?" is the question put to us by Mom.

It's a favorite ritual—the choosing of the next family adventure. We usually pick some awesome natural place in the United States. We've seen the Grand Canyon, Yellowstone, the giant redwoods of California, and more. But it doesn't have to be a famous touristy place. We are just as thrilled with simple things, and sharing our memories afterward is almost as good as the event itself.

"Remember the wheat fields of Nebraska?" one of us says.

"Remember the wild horses of Chincoteague?" says another.

"Yeah," we all murmur as we remember together.

"And how can we ever forget the Great Smoky Mountains?" Gramps adds. "They remind me of other mountains I saw when I was a boy. I've tried to paint them several times, but I'm never entirely satisfied with the result. I can't seem to find the blue that's in my head—in the mind's eye of my memory."

"Anyhow . . ." Mom jolts us back to the present. "Where to this summer?"

"Niagara Falls!" The words burst out of Gramps, like he's been holding them in forever. Nobody has a better suggestion, so we agree on Niagara. We begin planning immediately—when to leave, what to take, what to wear.

On Saturday Mom takes me and David into town with her. She has errands to run, and she suggests that David and I walk to the video store while she's in the supermarket. She wants a travel video about Niagara Falls.

"Rent something fun too!" Mom calls as we leave her in the parking lot.

I'm in high spirits as we walk down the street. There's a hint of lilacs on the air. A brilliant sun dances on display windows. Some of the townspeople speak to us. A large floppy-eared dog grins at us.

"Meggie! David!"

We turn to see old Mr. Bleep sitting on a bench across the street in front of the post office. Kids started calling him Mr. Bleep because his real name sounds like a bad word that's off-limits to us. Over time, the adults have picked up the nickname too.

We like Mr. Bleep. You might call him our local character. He hangs around town and strikes up conversations with anybody who will talk to him. A few years back he suffered a stroke, which left him with a weird vision problem—he sees dead people, or so he claims.

"Come sit," he invites us, patting the bench beside him.

"For a minute?" I ask David.

"Why not?"

We cross the street and sit on the bench beside Mr. Bleep.

"Such a day for aliens!" he says in his friendly way, before we can ask how he is.

Oh, no. Aliens again? My high spirits take a nosedive.

"Aliens?" David says, and glances at me. "What about them?"

"One of my little friends, Kitty Singer—you know Kitty, don't you, Meggie?"

"Yeah."

"Well, a few minutes ago she was talking to me about the aliens."

I try to laugh. "That Kitty! And did she tell you how they suck your soul out through your big toe?"

But Mr. Bleep does not laugh. He nods slowly and looks toward the sky.

"I don't know how they do it," he says in all seriousness. "But they do steal souls. They want to take over the earth. It's no laughing matter."

"Don't you think that's a bit far-fetched?" David teases Mr. Bleep. "People from outer space?"

"Not far-fetched at all," Mr. Bleep responds.

All three of us turn our eyes to the sky.

Mr. Bleep adjusts his glasses. "Did I ever tell y'all about my vision problem?"

We nod.

"It's not that I can't see," he insists. "I can see as good as I did before the stroke—just about, anyhow—but now I can also see spots everywhere, and glare, and clouds floating about the edges." He moves his hand around his head as he speaks.

"That must be aggravating," I say.

"It is, child. It's definitely aggravating. That's the word, all right."

"Do you still see ghosts, Mr. Bleep?" David asks.

"Yeah, I saw my dear mom and dad only yesterday, and them dead these many years. But that ain't all," he adds.

"What do you mean?" David says.

"Well, most folks laugh at me, but I'm used to it by now," Mr. Bleep says sadly, and I understand that he really is not used to it at all. "Nobody believes me. They think I'm just a senile old man. Maybe I am."

"We'll believe you, Mr. Bleep," David says.

"Just lately I've been seeing aliens," Mr. Bleep goes on. "I don't see them all the time, and they don't talk to me or nothing like that. They're just there."

"But not really there?" I say hopefully, twisting my hands nervously.

Mr. Bleep shrugs. "Who knows? I've read up on strokes and how they sometimes affect your eyesight. It's the brain, see, and not the eyes, that's damaged. If they could find a way to fix the brain after a stroke, it would take care of the vision problem. Anyhow, I started seeing these aliens in the clouds floating around in my field of vision."

"What do they look like?" David asks.

"Some of them are tall and skinny with big liquid slanting eyes. Others look just like you and me."

If some of the aliens look like us, then how can he be sure they *are* aliens? I start to ask Mr. Bleep that question, but something is happening to the conduit between my brain and my vocal cords, and I suddenly find myself babbling insanely in a screechy high-pitched voice.

For as long as I can remember, I've had to put up with this thing. It happens most often when I'm overanxious. You don't want to know how folks look at me when I flip out this way—like I'm a real flake. At one time David had the same disorder, but being the perfect kid he is, he outgrew it.

One time I heard a teacher referring to me as "the girl with Tourette's." Another time a neighbor called it "the most abnormal stutter" she'd ever heard. That made my face burn, but I knew this was not Tourette's and not a stutter. It was something else entirely. The middle school principal recommended therapy for my "speech defect," but Mom would have none of it.

"There's nothing wrong with her," Mom told him. "It's just a nervous tic that runs in our family. I'll work with her myself."

She did that very thing, and in time I learned to control my outbursts to some degree, but on this day I find myself losing it again. I know all the talk about aliens has something to do with it.

David yanks my arm hard and practically yells, "We gotta go!"

Finally I clap my free hand over my runaway mouth and end the tirade. David pulls me to my feet. Mr. Bleep has struggled to a standing position also, and now gapes at me.

"What kind of gibberish was that?" he cries, but David is dragging me away.

As we leave, I see that Mr. Bleep's pale knobby hands have started to flutter.

We hurry across the street, and David whispers to me, "We can't take you anywhere, can we?"

"Let go of me!" With one mighty jerk, I manage to wrench myself free of him.

David takes off like he's going to put out a fire, and I have to run to keep up with him. At the video store he acts like I'm some stray he can't shake. I find a documentary about Niagara, and we each choose one movie for fun. My pick is *Marley & Me*. I love any movie or book about dogs. Mom and Gramps have promised me a golden retriever puppy for my birthday this summer.

Mr. Alvarez, who manages the video store, rings up our selections and tosses a box of microwave popcorn into the plastic bag along with the videos. "Enjoy a treat with your movies tonight."

"Sorry to decline," David says as he removes the popcorn, "but Mom didn't give us permission."

Mr. Alvarez throws back his head and laughs. " 'Sorry

to decline'?" he mocks David. "Leave it to this kid to use ten-dollar words, and to always mind Mom. The other young'uns around here just grab the grub and run."

With a tinge of satisfaction, I watch David's face go red. He doesn't know what to say. It's not the first time somebody has commented that his way of speaking is different. That's what he gets for being so proper. I know he can talk ordinary and even use slang when he wants to, so why doesn't he? Because he likes to put on airs.

"But it's free, child," Mr. Alvarez insists, and shoves the popcorn toward us again. "I'm giving a box to all my best customers today. Take it, and enjoy!"

David stands there thinking for a moment, then says in a mock Southern drawl, "Well, by cracky, in that case, my good feller, much obliged, much obliged!"

And in spite of being annoyed with David, I have to admit he does have a gift for impersonations. I would never tell him how good he is at it. Now his performance makes Mr. Alvarez laugh again. At the same time, we hear a siren from the street. Mr. Alvarez follows us out the door to see what's going on. Walking back the way we came, David and I see that an ambulance is parked in front of the post office across the street. Along with everyone else, we watch as someone on a stretcher is lifted into the rear of the vehicle.

Mr. O'Reilley, who delivers our mail, crosses the street and walks toward us.

"Who is it?" David calls to him.

The mailman glances behind him. "You mean on the

stretcher? It's Mr. Bleep, poor old guy. I'm no doctor, but it looks to me like he's had another stroke."

David and I gape at each other in astonishment.

"W-we were just talking to him," David sputters. "He seemed fine."

Mr. O'Reilley lays a sympathetic hand on David's shoulder.

"Sometimes these things come without warning, my lad. I'm sorry."

Then Mr. O'Reilley pats me on the head and moves on to continue with his deliveries. We watch the ambulance drive away with Mr. Bleep, before walking back to the parking lot to meet Mom. On the way home, we tell her all that happened.

· 3 ·

The next day David and I are playing basketball in the backyard when the county sheriff pulls his official car into our driveway, emerges in his spiffy blue uniform, and tips his hat to us. Sheriff DuBois is a pleasant-enough man, I suppose, but the sight of a uniformed officer always brings that echo back to me.

He goes to the back door and knocks. Mom, who is in the kitchen preparing lunch, invites him in. David and I drop the ball and go inside to see what's going on, and Gramps comes up from his workshop in the basement, where he's been tinkering.

Mom motions the sheriff toward the living room. "Will you sit with us?"

"Naw," the sheriff says as he props one foot on the bottom rung of a kitchen chair and removes his sunglasses.

"I won't keep you long. I want to ask your children some questions."

"David and Meggie?" Mom says, obviously surprised. She gestures for us to stand by her. "What about?"

David and I walk over to stand beside Mom.

"Well, I was informed that they were seen talking to Mr. Bleep yesterday right before he had a stroke." The sheriff looks at us. "Is that right, kids?"

"Yes," David responds. "We were talking to Mr. Bleep before we went to the video store, and when we came out again, the ambulance was there."

"Unfortunately, Mr. Bleep himself is not able to answer any questions right now," the sheriff says. "It seems he's had another stroke, but he may recover. In the meantime, maybe you can help me out. Can you tell me what you talked about?"

"Aliens," I blurt out. Mom lays a warm hand on my arm.

"What about aliens?" the sheriff inquires.

David and I by turns recount as much as we can remember of our conversation with Mr. Bleep, including his descriptions of the aliens.

"Hmmmm" is all the sheriff has to say as he scratches his head.

"Why do you need to know this, Sheriff DuBois?" Gramps asks.

"Just trying to put the puzzle together," the sheriff responds. "Mrs. Raskin told me she saw these kids talking to Mr. Bleep, and according to her, when they left him and crossed the street, Mrs. Raskin walked over to speak to him herself. When she got to where he was, she found Mr. Bleep to be in an agitated state. He was flailing his arms around and mumbling about alien kids. Then the stroke hit him. The Romano sisters said they saw it all from the post office window, and that it looked like Mr. Bleep was scared nearly to death."

I *don't* want to hear this. Because I know. I know it was my speech problem that scared poor Mr. Bleep. It may have caused his stroke. That makes me feel so bad. And did he think . . . ? Yes, he thought . . . He thought . . . Was he calling me and David *alien* kids?

"Well, it appears to me that the old man was having a senior moment," Gramps says.

"Yeah, it looks that way, but just 'cause he's old don't mean he's crazy."

"What do you mean?" Mom asks.

"I mean we've had these reports circulating for some months now, from many different sources, and a great flurry of them just lately."

"What reports?" Gramps says.

"Well, people say they've been seeing things, and they're scared."

"What things?" Gramps persists.

"Oh, you know, they're just your average alien sightings. I reckon people get on these kicks. Haven't you heard the UFO rumors?"

"I've heard!" Gramps snorts. "And I can't believe you're taking them seriously."

Mom laughs softly. "Aliens, Sheriff DuBois? Really, now . . ."

"I didn't say I'm a believer," the sheriff says, chuckling a little himself. "But I have to go through the motions. People are depending on me, you know."

"What did you expect to learn from the children?" Gramps asks.

"Anything that might give us a clue as to what scared the old man," the sheriff says. "It was Mrs. Raskin who suggested I come out here and talk to y'all."

"Mrs. Raskin?" I say. "But why?"

"Why indeed?" David says, unable to hide his irritation.

The sheriff chews on the earpiece of his sunglasses and studies David carefully for a time. Then he turns to Mom and says, "Your boy seems awful bright."

"Yes, quite bright," Mom agrees. "They both are."

"I mean, he has an unusual way of talking," the sheriff continues. "Around here you don't hear folks saying things like 'Why indeed?' Especially kids."

It's obvious that Mom is at a loss for words. She shrugs.

"Where was it y'all come from, up north somewhere?"

"California," Mom says. "But you see, their father— my late husband—grew up abroad. They both picked up idioms from him."

"Yeah, I reckon they would," the sheriff says.

"And both Meggie and David read a great deal as well," Mom adds. "I'm amazed sometimes at the expressions they pick up from their reading."

"Right," Sheriff DuBois says, and puts his sunglasses back on. "Anyhow, I'm awful sorry to bother y'all on a Sunday afternoon."

In a few minutes he's gone, leaving the four of us standing in our kitchen, just looking at each other, not knowing whether to laugh or cry.

That night I dream of an alien family who live in a round silver house high on a cliff among the clouds. And they have blue hair.

· 4 ·

It's officially the first day of summer, and I am at the front screen door trying to enjoy the smell of the summer rain. David is catching his daily show of man harassing alligator on Animal Planet. Gramps has been in his workshop for days, but today he has come upstairs to talk to Mom. I hear them whispering together on the front porch. They've been doing this a lot lately, and their secrecy really bugs me.

Our trip to Niagara Falls has been postponed for reasons unknown. Something wicked this way comes, but I am not in the loop to know about it.

"Why not just tell me and get it over with!" I suddenly yell, exasperated.

The whispering stops, and David clicks off the TV. Silently Mom and Gramps come inside, and the four of us scrunch up together on one couch. Gramps hugs me to him. Hanging on a cord around his neck is a silver object that looks like a long whistle.

"Yes, you're old enough to hear hard truths without falling apart," Gramps says.

"I am," I say, but my heart is thundering. "Tell me."

"It's all the talk in town—of aliens," Mom says softly.

"But what about it?" I say irritably.

"It grows worse and worse," Gramps says. "People are wild with fear. We must take precautions. Just in case . . . You know."

"What kind of precautions?"

"We must have a plan," Mom says.

I touch the whistle, and a vague memory stirs. We've had this thing for many years, and once it was used for . . . what? When?

"It's called the Log," Gramps says. "You were only three the last time we played it, and in case you've forgotten, it sounds like this." He props the whistle against his lips.

As he blows softly into it, a flimsy mist floats out of the air holes and circles our heads. It's gray and smells a lot like smoke, and there's another odor that's pretty bad, but I can't quite place it. At the same time this really lovely mystic music that sounds almost like a pan flute fills the house. I have to say, there's such a pang of longing and sadness in the sound that I feel like crying. I've almost remembered the last time I heard this whistle, when Gramps interrupts my thoughts.

"At full volume, it will be heard all around our property, and it's our danger signal," he says. "If you ever hear it, drop what you're doing and get to the basement pronto."

"We'll all meet there in Gramps's workshop," Mom says.

I can still smell the whistle mist, and feel the sadness in its music.

"And there we'll be safe from them?" I say.

"Utterly and completely," Gramps says. "They can't touch us there."

We fall asleep on the screened porch with moonlight washing over our faces. It's long after midnight when I wake up with a start, to the uncomfortable feeling of a hand being placed over my mouth.

Before I can react, Gramps whispers, "It's just me. Let's go quickly, quietly."

My body stiffens with fear.

When he takes his hand away from my mouth, I squeak, "Are they here?"

"Yes, in the cornfield."

I can't resist looking out at the corn in the full light of the moon. There I see dark figures moving without a sound among the stalks. I shrink against Gramps, fearing they might see us. But we have the advantage, for at this hour we are in the moon's shadow, and they are in its light.

I see Mom and David tiptoeing through the French doors into the house. With Gramps holding my hand, we follow.

In our bare feet we step down the stairs to the main floor, with Mom and David ahead of us. Nobody speaks as we hurry toward the basement stairs near the kitchen. Then I hear sounds outside the house, and my breath starts to come in gasps. Mom and David reach the basement stairs and disappear down them. When Gramps and I are inside the stairwell, he turns and locks the door behind us.

We hear something that sounds like angry growls outside our kitchen, and a thumping against the back door. I freeze in my tracks. Gramps scoops me up under one arm and carries me down the rest of the way. His workshop is enclosed within the full basement. Once inside this inner room, he sets me down and locks that door behind us.

And standing there before us is the Carriage. Shaped like a child's paper airplane, it has standing room of around seven feet, and an approximate width of eight feet at the base. The Carriage is also transparent, so that I can see Mom at the control panel and David on the floor behind her, against the wall. I step inside and crouch beside my brother.

Gramps follows and quickly secures the door of the Carriage. Mom points to a small computer screen and reads aloud to Gramps in our native tongue. Gramps looks at the screen, then begins working the controls.

The commotion I heard outside is now tumbling down the basement stairs, now pushing against the inner door. Terrified and fascinated at the same time, I watch that door while Gramps and Mom concentrate on the controls. Finally a little swoosh tells us the Carriage is in operation.

When the workshop door bursts open, I cry out. I

can't help myself. David clutches me to him, and I hold on.

Through the transparent walls, we can see clearly the faces of the townspeople surrounding the Carriage, and they can see us as well. Among others, we see Mrs. Raskin, Mr. Alvarez, Kitty's grandpa, the Romano sisters, Mr. O'Reilley—people we have grown to care about. But they have become a mob of strangers, and there is so much fear and anger and hate in their eyes that I hardly recognize them. Furiously they begin beating on the sides of the Carriage with sticks and stones and bare fists.

Then someone—Mr. O'Reilley, I think—grabs a hammer from Gramps's workbench and begins beating on the sides of the Carriage. Others take up heavy tools and do the same. Though the Carriage is soundproof, we still can hear muffled noises. The screams and curses get louder and louder and more ferocious as the people hammer the sides.

Gramps is frantic as he strikes the palm of his hand against a wide bar, which reads in English: OPEN THE GATE.

Instantly the Carriage is enveloped in a white vapor. The Gate has opened for us, and like a spear cutting through water, we move swiftly through it, to safety on the other side.

· 5 ·

David Speaks

According to legend, at the dawn of time, in the distant world of Chroma, when the life-forms there were not highly evolved, much of the planet was shrouded in darkness. During those dark periods, luminescent streaks began to appear, as if by magic, in the hair of the planet's inhabitants, who were my ancestors.

For females the color was a whimsical periwinkle, and for males a deep royal blue. The streaks were attractive, and both shades glowed in the dark, though they could appear in daylight as well. Subsequently, our race, for eons, was known by a Chroma word meaning "blue."

That's the reason my mother chose the name Blue for herself, and for me and my sister, Meggie, when we traveled from our homeland of Chroma to Earth.

In a more enlightened age, Chromian anthropologists studied the phenomenon of the blue hair and declared that, in the beginning, its main purpose was to help the people identify one another in the dark, but it was also apparent that a person did not begin to glow until he or she had come to a certain degree of maturity in body, mind, and spirit. Most Chromians were proud to reach this plateau around the age of twelve, give or take a year, but some rare individuals, sadly, never arrived. I achieved blue at the age of eleven, but Meggie, being very immature in many ways, did not.

Once, our home planet was a land of many bright colors, thus the name Chroma, but by the time Meggie and I were born, it had become a bleak and dying world, with its air, soil, and water contaminated beyond salvation. In fact, pollution poisoning killed off our people in great numbers, with Dad and Grandmama being among those who perished.

Though Chroma's technology was highly sophisticated, our fine scientists could not reverse the damage done to the environment. Attempting to make amends for this dismal failure, they developed the ultimate vehicle for dimensional and space travel—the Carriage. This grand creation was unique in that it was programmed to seek out the hidden passages and secret gateways of the universe, making it possible for its occupants to navigate astronomical distances in short periods of time.

With the Carriage, Chromians could leave the sad ruins of our once-splendid civilization and migrate in small groups to other, more promising worlds, where we could assimilate undetected into society.

Mom and Gramps chose Earth for its natural beauty,

and the United States of America for its magnificent Constitution. The English language was also a plus. Mom learned it as a child from her teacher, who had learned it from his space travels. Mom taught English to Gramps, then to me and Meggie, along with Chromish, when we first began to speak.

As for our bodies, it was always a mystery to me why Earthlings imagined that someone alien to their planet would have to be grotesque. In Chroma kindergarten I learned that advanced life is similar all over the universe, except for some rare mutations on the far edges of the known galaxies. In fact, the major difference in appearance we found between ourselves and the Earthlings was size. Chromian adults were, on the average, about six inches shorter than Earthlings, and weighed much less. A petite figure was considered a trait of beauty and was desired by both men and women.

After much debate and soul-searching, Mom requested the services of Chroma's physicians, who were among the most skilled in the universe, to treat each of us with growth enzymes, so that we would not be considered oddities among the natives of Earth. Mom and Gramps assumed these new bodies with great misgivings, because they seemed, as Meggie's friend Kitty Singer might say, "Ooo-ooo, gross!" In only a matter of months, the change was complete and permanent. Meggie and I were too young to care very much, soon forgetting how we had looked before, and the adults, out of necessity, learned, in time, to adjust.

I was five and Meggie three when we arrived in the

Carriage on the shores of California, USA, North America, Earth, expecting to find security and happiness—as we surely did for a time. Through all the amazing years of living on Earth, we did not speak of our secret even with each other, but harbored it close to our hearts. At times it seemed Meggie might have forgotten Chroma completely, and it was best, I thought, if she could forget who we really were. But I was wrong. She remembered much more than I suspected. In fact, I thought perhaps her memories of Chroma and the attack of the madman created her fears of being hunted like an animal.

Now here we are once again, homeless. The Carriage, however, cuts through the blackness with such stunning sureness that I feel strangely safe. If somebody were out there watching our flight, this superb vehicle might appear to be a glass rocket. But of course it's not glass at all. It's made from a fine and complex synthetic, unknown on Earth.

A dim light from the control panel allows us to see each other, and the Carriage temperature is perfectly regulated so that we are comfortable. Mom and Gramps appear almost to be in shock. They are still standing at the controls, but not touching anything, just staring ahead. Meggie and I sit huddled together against the wall. Far off we can see sporadic twinkles of light in the vast, cold blackness around us.

"We meant them . . . no harm. . . . We meant them . . . no harm," Mom mumbles. "We wanted only to live, to survive, to raise healthy children on their lovely planet. We were good citizens. How could they . . . ?"

For a while there is no sound but the hum of the Carriage.

"Where are we going, Gramps?" I whisper.

"I don't know," Gramps says, and gazes out into the nothingness.

"You don't know?" Meggie says.

"I'll be perfectly honest with you," Gramps says. "I was in such a panic, you understand, so desperate to get away from those . . . those . . ."

"Those *maniacs*!" I finish for him, and Mom doesn't scold me.

Remembering the hate-filled faces of the Earthlings who broke into our home, I shiver. Even Kitty's grandpa! I'm sure that hurt Meggie's feelings.

"I'm so sorry," Gramps whispers at last. "I don't know where we're going. I remember entering a command for a place where the English language is spoken."

"Do you think there is such a place, other than Earth?" says Mom.

"I don't know," Gramps says. "Perhaps another Earth in a parallel universe?"

"Perhaps," Mom agrees.

"Next I requested a secluded landing site," Gramps continues. "Then we were surrounded by those . . . those . . . eyes . . . those faces!" Gramps's voice trembles as he speaks. "I was so alarmed, I'm not sure what commands I entered after that."

"It's all right, Dad," Mom says sweetly. "You saved our lives."

Meggie and I murmur agreement.

"I should have studied the tutorial more thoroughly when I had time," Mom says. "But I guess I was hoping we would never have to use the Carriage again. I thought we were settled for life."

Mom and Gramps sit down against the wall with me and Meggie, and we watch the distant twinkles. As we each slip into our own private fears and imaginings, a great pall of wretchedness settles over us.

It seems hours later that Mom brings forth clothes she has stashed under the control panel.

"I have jeans, T-shirts, caps, shoes, and socks for all of us," she says. "I placed them here a few days ago in case we had to leave in a hurry—which, as it turns out, we did."

In the dim light we turn our backs to each other and change clothes quickly. For the time being we don't put on shoes. Mom stuffs our pajamas into a backpack, and we settle against the wall again.

"Why didn't they like us?" Meggie asks sadly. "Especially when we liked them so much?"

"They were afraid," Gramps says. "Earthlings have an unreasonable fear of the unknown."

"Why can't we go back and live in another state where nobody knows us?" Meggie goes on.

"Yes. Nebraska, maybe," I say eagerly. "Or Oregon."

"Alaska!" Meggie adds.

"I'm afraid not," Gramps says. "You realize, don't you, that within hours our faces will be on every television screen, every magazine cover, and every newspaper on Earth?"

"CNN is probably at the old Fischer place already," Meggie says.

"It will become a tourist attraction," Mom adds, smiling a bit.

"Maybe my paintings will sell!" Gramps says, and we laugh out loud.

"Well, before we get to wherever we're going," Mom says with a great sigh, "we must record our memories of Earth. We may never see that fine planet again, so we don't want to forget anything important."

Gramps tugs the Log from under his T-shirt and places it between his thumb and index finger. He raises it to his mouth and begins to blow softly. Mom snaps on another light so that we can see the whistle mist. This unique musical instrument came with us from our own native and ancient planet. In fact, during our trip to Earth from Chroma, we used it to store memories of the home we were leaving.

"So we won't completely forget who we are," Mom told us then.

Presently its nostalgic murmurings fill the Carriage. We close our eyes and share the same memories of living on Chroma when Meggie and I were very young. There we are in our small bodies, and the adults proudly displaying their fluorescent-streaked hair. But the mist is gray and foul-smelling because that was our planet's condition at the time of our departure. With the help of the Log, we remember with awful clarity the ravaged forests and rivers, the wasted mountains and valleys.

Then all else melts away as the spirit of my father moves among us. We can feel his strength and his love. In fact, he is so real, I gasp and reach out a hand for him, but he is gone. I can hear Mom sniffing.

Gramps takes the whistle away from his lips. "Now express what you want to remember from Earth," he says softly. "We'll all concentrate on that memory, and it'll be saved forever." He resumes playing the music.

"The swallows coming back to Capistrano," Meggie says dreamily.

We all murmur agreement and remember.

Golden retrievers. Strawberries. Spring.

An azure mist curls from the Log, encircling our heads. It smells of Earth's wind and briny seas. A green mist follows. It smells of wild mint, cut grass, and more, much more.

We remember swimming, playing basketball, watching videos, the old Fischer place.

Meggie takes a deep breath and says the name of Kitty Singer. The rest of us tactfully don't mention the role Kitty's grandpa played in driving us away from Earth. We help Meggie remember Kitty as the cool kid she is, as we add her to the other wonders of the world we have left behind. We store them all in the Log.

Then Mom takes the Log from Gramps, so that he can add his own memories to ours. She plays with an aching sweetness.

"The smell of October," Gramps says. "Let's never forget that!"

Yeah, Halloween. And snow. And Christmas.

On and on we remember, while spearing through space in our crystal-clear rocket, as the Log records the sights and smells of Earth.

Wild geese. Sleeping in the moonlight. Fireflies.

Blue hills.

· 6 ·

Back to Meggie

I hear Gramps whispering. "It's a kind of gazebo."
When the music of the Log put me to sleep, I
dreamed of Kitty in the strawberry patch, and her voice
still echoes in my head: *All good things start with a dream.*

I sit up and look out. Yes, it's night, but I can see that
we have landed beside a gazebo in what looks like a public park.

Now David is sitting up too.

"Make haste," Mom whispers. "Put on your shoes and
socks. We must get out and dismantle the Carriage before we're sighted."

We are quick but quiet. Gramps unsnaps the control
panel from the Carriage wall. Mom folds it up to the size
of a book and places it inside the backpack. Then we step
outside. The air is warm.

It's a nice park. The trees, shrubbery, and grass are well

cared for. There are picnic tables, barbecue grills, and playground equipment. I see a far pale moon and scattered stars. We can see tall buildings silhouetted against the night sky a short distance away.

Mom and Gramps together pull dowels from crucial points of the Carriage, until it collapses at our feet. I'm reminded of the melting of the witch in *The Wizard of Oz*, when Dorothy throws water on her. What's left of the Carriage is a heap of material as fine as silk. Mom picks it up and shakes it out; then, with each of us taking a corner, we fold it like a very large sheet. This and the dowels are placed inside the backpack with the control panel. Gramps removes the Log from around his neck and tucks it in as well. Then he shoulders the pack and moves toward the city, motioning to us to stay behind him.

At the park entrance both Gramps and Mom hesitate. We stand still in the dark, looking at the city. It could be any city in America, except that there are few streetlights and no traffic. In fact, there's not a sign of life.

"Perhaps we should wait until daylight to go into the city," Mom whispers. "Then we can blend in with the natives as we did on arriving in California."

We agree.

We can barely make out words on the archway over the entrance.

FASHION CITY PARK
A GIFT TO THE PEOPLE FROM THE FATHERS

"English!" Gramps exclaims with relief.

He herds us back into the park, where we settle down on the grass behind some shrubbery to wait for daylight. Soon my head is resting on Mom's lap. The silence of the place is deafening. Not a car horn, train whistle, siren, or airplane. Not a single voice, or a barking dog.

David breaks the stillness. "Gramps, you said Earthlings fear the unknown."

"That's right," Gramps says.

"But how did they know we were from another world? For the most part, we managed to hide our differences from them."

"Yeah," I say. "What gave us away?"

"Oh, I don't know," Gramps says. "Maybe blue hair?"

David loves reminding me that he wasn't quite eleven when he achieved blue, but here I am almost twelve and I haven't yet.

"But don't worry about it, Meggie," he has said to me several times. "People are different, and I think Chromian boys, as a group, grow up faster than girls."

I could just barf when he says that. And now I have this new fear to add to all the others. What if I never achieve blue? Some few Chromians don't.

Then I'm back and forth. Maybe, being in another world, I'm lucky not to have to deal with it.

And back and forth. But all Chromians know it's a mark of maturity. Who doesn't want to grow up?

Anyway, on Earth, Mom discovered that vinegar solves the problem of the blue streaks. She explained to me that somehow the chemical reaction between Earth vinegar and these metallic elements from Chroma neutralizes the color, so that it dissolves. Since nobody knows when the streaks might pop up, we have learned to routinely check heads before leaving home. We also carry some kind of head covering with us wherever we go, and when practical, we carry small vials of vinegar in our pockets.

Still we were not always successful in hiding that particular secret from Earthlings. David was sent home from school more than once for having "weird paint" in his hair.

"Yeah, my Gramps is an artist," David told his teacher one time.

Later, in recounting the story to us, David said that he turned to his classmates at that point and teased them.

"Well, at least it's only paint, and not something worse!"

He was referring to the fact that some of them had recently been sent home for head lice. Of course everybody laughed. And that's how things have always gone for David. Even though other kids are just as put out with his everlasting perfection as I am, when he decides to charm you, he gets away with it.

"Having a kid who babbles a Blue streak might have tipped them off too," Mom adds with a laugh. "Pardon the pun."

Since David and I learned English and Chromish at the same time, both of us used to get so mixed up sometimes that we swapped words and sounds of the two languages back and forth. Sometimes we had to stop and think if a word was Chromish or English. But some of Chromish sounds way different from any Earth language because it has tongue clicks in it, and lip whistles, even some gurgles and other throat sounds. I'm sure it must sound funny to an Earthling. That would explain why one person thought I had Tourette's syndrome! And another thought I had a bad stutter. Mr. Bleep simply called it gibberish.

David, naturally, never gets his languages mixed up anymore. In fact, I don't think he even remembers Chromish. But Chromish is much better for expressing yourself. So when I get nervous, all those clicks and whistles and gurgles come automatically.

"What about a kid who talks like a professor?" I say, trying not to sound peevish.

"That's not a trait unknown to Earthlings," Mom says.

"People were always saying what a brain David is," I go on, "but you know what? It actually annoyed the other kids, and grown-ups thought he was odd."

David shrugs. "They just thought I was a nerd," he says. "So what? Bill Gates was a nerd too. Anyway, I think Mrs. Raskin started all the talk about us. She thought Meggie and I had something to do with Mr. Bleep's stroke. The other day she actually cornered me at the drugstore and said, 'Y'all can't fool me, boy. Mr. Bleep found out something about you Blues, didn't he? He called you alien kids! Alien kids!'"

We laugh, because David is talking through his nose, and he sounds just like Mrs. Raskin—real witchy and gossipy.

"But they had no substantial evidence to support their suspicions," Mom says. "Not until they actually saw us in the Carriage, ready to escape."

"Perhaps they assumed we were aliens because I told them so," Gramps says.

"You told!"

After a long sigh, Gramps makes his confession. "It was the day I went to the barbershop to get a haircut. The place was full of geezers—you know the ones who hang out there all the time. But it was that old busybody Henry Singer who was running his mouth the most. He was talking when I went in. He didn't see me."

"Kitty's grandpa?" I exclaim. "What did he say?"

" 'Them dirty aliens out at the old Fischer place musta done something pretty creepy to give poor old Bleep a stroke' is what he said. 'I say we don't need their kind around here.' That's all I heard, but it was enough to provoke my wrath."

"And you just had to respond!" Mom scolds him. "You couldn't drop it."

"Naturally I had to defend my family. So I said, 'You're right, Henry. We are aliens from a dying world, and we came to Earth to get away from a great big stink, but now that I've met you, I guess we'll have to move again!' "

"You did not!" I cry out.

"I'm afraid I did. I thought everybody would take it as a joke and laugh about it, and that would be the end of it," Gramps says. "Because you know, sometimes truth is stranger than fiction, and when you put it out there bluntly, it sounds so outrageous, you have to laugh at yourself for ever believing such a thing. At least, that was my theory. I never dreamed they would take me seriously. Actually, a few of them did laugh, but most didn't even crack a smile. And they sat there staring at me with their mouths hanging open.

"That's when I caught my reflection in one of the mirrors, and right there above my left ear, shining brightly for all the world to see, was a strand of hair as royal blue as a king's robe!"

"No way!" I cry.

"Way," Gramps says without enthusiasm. "Way indeed. You see, once before, Bob the barber commented on a small blue spot at my temple, and I used the same excuse David used at school. I told him it was paint, and he believed me then, but this time I could see that that explanation wouldn't fly.

"That's when I said to them, 'So, can I expect you gentlemen to come at midnight and burn a cross in my yard?'

"But they said not a word, and I left quickly. As I was walking back to my car, I could feel their eyes on me, and I did not like the sensation. I think that's when and where the plot for vigilante activity was hatched."

"What do you think they would have done to us," David asks, "had they been able to lay hands on us?"

Nobody answers, and we huddle close against the night air.

· 7 ·

A thick haze hangs over the land, so that daylight doesn't wake us. But a police officer with a nightstick does.

"Did you spend the night in the park?"

We scramble to our feet, brush off our clothes, and smooth them with nervous fingers.

The officer is tall and muscular. His hair, poking out from under his hat, is blond, his eyes blue. His uniform is similar to ones we've seen before. On his shoulder patch are the words *Fashion City Police Department*. His face is a study in bewilderment.

"G-good morning, sir." Gramps stutters a bit.

I become aware of sounds from the city.

"Morning to you!" the officer returns the greeting. "Where do you come from?"

This question is directed at Gramps, and he doesn't know what to say. He clears his throat, glances behind him, jerks his head in the direction of the gazebo, and mumbles, "Back there."

"Oh! You have escaped from the Western Province?" the cop says with something like awe in his voice. "Really?"

I think he takes our silence for a yes.

"You're the third batch this year," the cop goes on. "And I have to say you all are looking pretty decent compared to the other ones. They were real beat-up and filthy dirty, having to walk all that way through the barbed wire and nasty weather, you know?"

After a pause, Mom says, "We managed to avoid both." Which is true.

"Well, good for you." The officer does a sharp turn on his heel, points to the city, and says, "Go down to the housing authority—it's the big red building on the right. There's a sign out front. They'll give you a place to live and some food and clothing rations. Tell them Officer Brent sent you."

"We cannot pay?" Gramps inflects his sentence so that it comes out like a question.

"Not to worry, my friend," Officer Brent says gently as he places a hand on Gramps's arm. "The Fathers take care of the people here."

After all we've been through, I don't know why this cop makes me feel like crying by saying something nice. But I don't cry. It seems Mom, Gramps, and David are also touched. We glance around at the bushes and the trees.

"Is there work to be had?" Gramps asks.

"Of course. The people at the housing authority will

direct you to the employment agency, the food market, the mall—wherever you need to go."

"Thank you kindly, sir," Gramps says as he shoulders the backpack.

"Just one more thing," Officer Brent says as he unclips a metal device from his waistband. "I have to check your bag for weapons. Just a precaution."

Oh, no, no. He'll find the Carriage. I look at Mom. She looks back at me with wide eyes. David is nervously moving his hands in and out of his pockets. Gramps just seems helpless. He hands the pack over to the policeman.

Officer Brent pushes a button on his device and a beam of light shoots out. He runs the light carefully over the backpack. We hear a faint buzz, but no alarm bells and no terrifying words such as "Put your hands above your heads" from the officer.

"All clear" is what he says, and that with a smile on his face. "Welcome to Fashion City, good folks. You'll like it here. Everybody does."

He hands the backpack to Gramps, turns on his heel, and leaves us alone. We all let out our breath and look at each other.

"I was sure he was going to open it," Mom says as she slumps against a tree. "My knees are shaking."

"How easy was that?" David says, grinning. "We're home free."

Gramps shoulders the backpack. "We'll see. Housing authority, first stop."

After a quick head check, Mom says, "I put the vinegar

vials in our jeans pockets in case we need them, and I have baseball caps for everybody in the backpack. But let's not wear the caps right now. Let's wait to see if they're appropriate in this place."

For the second time we walk to the park entrance and look out at the street. Now we see a real city, bustling with cars, buses, taxis, pedestrians.

As we walk down the street, the police officer's hokey words echo in my head and comfort me. *The Fathers take care of the people here.*

Lots of people are friendly and say good morning to us. We crane our necks as tourists might do, but I don't see anything unusual here. There's a street, sidewalks and curbs, brick buildings, stone buildings, wooden buildings, different kinds of vehicles, traffic lights, benches at bus stops, advertisements. Everything seems kinda outdated, but for a city, it'll do, I guess.

Several large billboards advertising a product called Lotus catch our eye.

TAKE IT FOR A HEADACHE OR A HEARTACHE.
JUST ONE LOTUS FOR A DIFFERENCE YOU WILL NOTICE!

A HOLIDAY CAN BLOAT US,
AND THAT'S WHY WE REACH FOR LOTUS!

TAKE LOTUS IF YOU'RE TIRED
LOTUS IF YOU'RE FIRED
AND SOON YOU'LL BE REHIRED!

Ahead of us and towering over the street is the largest billboard of them all. We stop in our tracks to look at this smiling twenty-foot-tall family—mother, father, boy, girl—seated in front of a television set, obviously engrossed in the show they are watching. The caption reads:

THE FAMILY HOUR
ENTERTAINMENT FOR THE WHOLE FAMILY
EACH NIGHT AT 8:30
PRESENTED BY THE FATHERS

"Isn't it lovely?" someone says, and we turn to see a small older lady dressed neatly in gray. She has paused beside Mom to study the billboard.

I can see that Mom is weighing her response. I know for a fact that she has never considered any billboard lovely. She thinks they are eyesores, and this one is bigger than most. But, hey, this is a whole new world, and it's our first day.

"Quite lovely indeed," Mom says.

"And it serves as a gentle reminder to each of us on our way to work each day," the gray lady says.

"A reminder?" Gramps says.

"A reminder of all the things the Fathers have done for us!" the woman gushes.

"Quite so!" Gramps agrees with her heartily.

The woman waves a small hand at us and continues on her way. The four of us look at each other with questions in our eyes, then move on.

"Hey, there are some kids with baseball caps on," David comments. "I wonder if they have logos on them for certain teams."

But as we draw near, we can see that the caps are plain like ours, or they have some dumb slogan like *Praise the Fathers*. Still, it's good to see that baseball caps, jeans, and T-shirts are in.

Soon we find ourselves in front of a red building on which a sign reads: FASHION CITY HOUSING AUTHORITY. We enter.

Inside is a large office with some employees working at computers; others are talking on the phone. A smiling middle-aged woman at the first station stands up to greet us. The badge attached to her navy blouse reads, HI! MY NAME IS AMANDA HARP.

Amanda Harp seems about to bubble over with good cheer. "May I help you?"

"Officer Brent sent us here to apply for housing," Mom says to the woman.

"Is something wrong with your current quarters?" Amanda coos.

"We just arrived," Mom says, "from . . ."

I know what Mom is thinking. It seems ridiculous to say we have come from the Western Province when we really don't know where it is, or *what* it is.

But Gramps jumps right in there. "We escaped from the Western Province!"

One of Amanda's hands flies to her heart. "Is that right!" She is so bowled over, she can't say another word at the moment. Then, collecting herself, she narrows her hazel eyes and leans in close to whisper, "Are people really eating rats over there?"

David and I exchange significant glances. Eating rats?

"What sort of accommodations can we expect?" Mom tries to change the subject.

But Amanda will not be sidetracked. "From the Western Province. I declare!" she says, looking at us with awe on her face. It seems she can't get over it. "Is it really as gross as they say?"

"We prefer not to talk about it," Mom says softly, and she's totally believable.

"Oh, yes, of course! Of course!" Amanda comes to her senses and quickly begins a search on her computer. "Now, let me see," she muses aloud. "Two adults and two children—a girl and a boy. We have a three-bedroom, two-bath available in Sector B, Building 9, Apartment 603. I just need to get some information first. Names and ages?"

"I am sixty years old!" Gramps lies with confidence, shaving off five years, as usual. "My name is Sam Lane. This is my daughter, Linda Blue, a widow, age thirty-seven, and her two children, Meggie, eleven, and David, thirteen."

"And the season of each birthday?"

The season? It's a strange question, but one by one we answer, and Amanda enters the data into her computer.

"Escaped from Western Province," she says aloud as she enters that information as well. Then she turns back to us and gives us her brightest smile. "The apartment is furnished with everything you need—furniture, dishes, linens, you name it. You'll find directions to Sector B at the bus stop. Welcome to Fashion City, Mr. Lane, Mrs. Blue, Meggie, and David. I'm sure you'll like it here. Everybody does."

"What about employment?" Gramps asks. "Officer Brent said jobs are available?"

"That's very true," Amanda Harp chirps. "You need to go to the employment agency to apply. It's the brick building just up the street."

"Officer Brent also said something about food and clothing rations," Mom says.

"Certainly! Where is your head, Amanda?" Amanda chides herself. Then she tears two sheets of what look like postage stamps from a black book. "This ought to do until your first payday. And if you're hungry now, you can use them at any restaurant."

Mom takes the stamps and thanks Amanda.

"Oh, don't thank me. Thank the Fathers!" Amanda says.

· 8 ·

Outside, the sun has burned off much of the smog. Mom points to the only brick building in sight and says, "The employment office."

We walk down the street, and Gramps puts an arm around my shoulders. "Hungry, Meggie B.?"

"I could eat a pizza the size of a piano."

"Well, maybe we can find one when we're done at the employment agency."

I guess this won't be so bad. The people certainly seem happy. We can start all over again here in the city, and perhaps later find a home in the countryside.

At the Fashion City employment agency there's a small stoop in front of the door, with five steps leading up to it. In the window is a sign—NO CHILDREN ALLOWED.

Mom and Gramps look at me and David, then at each other.

"You go in first and I'll stay with the kids," Mom says to Gramps.

"We're not babies, you know!" David says. "We can stay out here alone."

"We don't know anything about this place," Mom argues. "I prefer not to leave you unsupervised."

"They will be perfectly safe, madam," comes a big booming voice, and there is Officer Brent walking up behind us, twirling his nightstick. His face is red, and wet with sweat, but he is smiling. "We proudly proclaim ourselves the safest city on the planet."

"On the *whole* planet?" I speak up, hoping he will say which planet we're on.

"Yes, the safest city on the whole planet. No violent crime, no poverty, no disease."

Then he turns to Mom and Gramps and says, "Go on now, both of you. If you're concerned, I'll stay close by until you're through in there."

"Well, all right," Mom agrees reluctantly, with a bit of worry in her eyes. Then to me and David she says, "Stay where I can see you when I look out the window, okay?"

Mom and Gramps disappear into the building, and David and I sit down on the top step to wait.

"I'll be walking up and down this sidewalk," Officer Brent tells us, and strolls away.

We watch people passing. Many of them smile or speak to us. A young couple alternately talk and pant as they jog. Several people ride by on bicycles. I have to say it's a right pleasant and peaceful scene.

"No crime, no poverty, no disease," David says as we watch the people.

"That doesn't seem likely, does it?" I say.

"No crime and no poverty I suppose is possible," he says. "But no disease?"

We puzzle on that one until our thoughts are interrupted by a big white bus lumbering down the street. There are purple letters stenciled on the side, proudly proclaiming that this is

VACATION 65!

The gray heads tell us that old people occupy this bus. They are waving and calling out as they move down the street. It's nice to see old people happy and excited about going on vacation.

Many passersby stop to wave at the people on the bus. So we wave too.

"Goodbye! Goodbye!"

Vacation 65 halts at a bus stop where a man with a shiny bald head is waiting. It appears that his children and grandchildren have come to see him off. All of them laugh and cry as they hug him.

"Have a wonderful time!"

"Praise the Fathers!"

"Farewell, Grandpapa. Farewell!"

But suddenly the man clutches a young woman, probably his daughter, clings to her, and cries like I did on my first day of school. It looks like this grandpapa does not want to go on vacation without his family. The woman reassures him, and eventually he settles down, steps onto the bus, and doesn't turn back. We can see the other seniors greeting him. As the bus moves on, the family members wipe their eyes and drift away.

"Will you look at that!" David cries suddenly.

My eyes follow David's, and there walking toward us on the sidewalk is this guy who looks for all the world like a young Elvis Presley. He's wearing a silky blue shirt and tight pants of the same material. He stops, takes his guitar out of its case, and then smiles and hums as he tunes up.

Officer Brent is nowhere in sight, and we leave the stoop, totally forgetting Mom's orders. When we come up close to Elvis, we can see a few coins already in his guitar case, which is lying open before him on the pavement.

I'm only vaguely aware of other people gathering around as Elvis starts picking and singing "Blue Suede Shoes." I notice he is actually *wearing* blue suede shoes. Suddenly it seems like he's singing just to me, and his mellow voice and curled lip make me weak.

"It *is* Elvis," David whispers to me.

It certainly is, and the up-close-and-personal Elvis is more gorgeous than any picture of him I've ever seen. I can dig how teens in the fifties lost their minds over him.

Other fans gather. Some people start clapping in time to the music. One young couple starts dancing. Elvis begins his famous hip rolls, which I have seen on old television shows a few times. I am so blown away that it takes me several minutes to realize that some of the people have started looking over their shoulders nervously. Then they begin to edge away from the scene, but I can tell they really want to stay.

My attention goes back to Elvis, and pretty soon I'm

breathlessly lost again in his magic spell. I have read that Elvis met Priscilla when she was only fourteen, and fell in love with her at first sight. Of course they didn't marry until she was twenty, but my point is this: suppose that on this Earth there is no Priscilla for him, but a Meggie instead?

That's when my sweet daydream is shattered by Officer Brent barging into the crowd waving a nightstick.

"Okay, break it up, folks!"

Elvis's audience vanishes just like that. Only David and I remain. Elvis, obviously frustrated, gives one last grating strum on his guitar, then places it inside the case and closes it up.

"What did I tell you I was going to do the next time I caught you performing in such a manner?" Officer Brent says to Elvis in a mean voice.

Elvis silently stretches forth both hands. The officer produces a pair of handcuffs, seemingly from nowhere, and snaps them into place around Elvis's wrists. My jaw drops. He's arresting Elvis Presley? A police cruiser pulls up to the curb, and Elvis is escorted toward it.

"You're a magnificent performer, Elvis!" The words burst suddenly from David. "Bravo!"

And he claps as hard as he can. I join him. Officer Brent scowls at us.

Elvis turns and gives us his famous cockeyed grin. "Thank you very much."

A curly lock of black hair falls over his forehead as he climbs into the backseat of the police cruiser. Hastily David picks up the guitar in its case where it remains on the sidewalk and places it at Elvis's feet in the car. Then Officer Brent closes the car door, and Elvis is hauled away.

Puzzled, I stand with David and Officer Brent, watching the patrol car drive away.

"Why was he arrested?" David asks, obviously irked.

"You saw him, and heard him!" Officer Brent growls. "And still you ask me that?" He stands sternly with hands on hips, glaring at David. "And furthermore," he scolds, "I don't like your tone or your attitude, young man! You should not have clapped for him. I know you are from a savage place, and your ignorance is your excuse, but now you have been warned. Okay?"

When David speaks again, his face is red, but his tone is more polite. "But if you please, sir, that was Elvis."

"Yeah, I think that's his name. Elvis Preston—or something like that."

"What were the charges?" I speak up.

"Gross uniqueness, of *course*!" Officer Brent exclaims, as if I should know this. "And of the worst kind too!"

Gross uniqueness? Is he kidding?

"What do you suppose would happen if we let that go on and never tried to put a stop to it?" Officer Brent asks.

We cannot imagine.

"I'll tell you what! Next thing you know, others would have those revolting sideburns! And . . . and be scavenging silk clothes and blue shoes from God knows where. And they'd be singing catchy songs in the streets and wiggling in time to the music!"

The man is serious.

"And there's no telling what that might lead to," Officer Brent goes on. "Other dark and dangerous things, I'm sure. It's a terrible influence on children like you. Just terrible! Now mind your mom and go back to the stoop."

Officer Brent abruptly turns from us and continues walking his beat. David and I plod back to perch on the steps and wait for Mom and Gramps. A long silence ensues, until at last David turns to me and says, "Toto, I don't think we're in Kansas anymore."

· 9 ·

"We saw Elvis Presley!" David and I shout as Mom and
Gramps come out of the employment agency. We're practically jumping up and down with excitement, but they're
not one bit impressed.

Mom takes the time to fold up a piece of paper and
tuck it into a back pocket of her jeans before saying, "It's
almost lunchtime, and I know you must be hungry."

"Yes, we should find a place to eat," Gramps agrees.

Mom and Gramps start walking toward the busier part
of the city, leaving us to trail behind. Sometimes they just
don't listen.

"Mom! Gramps! We're not kidding!" I cry. "We *really*
saw Elvis Presley in person!"

That does the trick. Both Gramps and Mom stop and
stare at me.

"He wasn't an impersonator?" Mom says.

"No!" we say.

"I don't think so," David adds.

"He looked like the real thing to me," I say. "And his name was Elvis."

"And he was young," David says. "About twenty or so."

Mom is frowning, and Gramps rubs the top of his balding head, muttering.

"Keep it under your hats for now," Mom says. "We want to hear all about it over lunch."

Just down the street we find a sandwich shop called—what else? The Sandwich Shop. The menu is simple: hot dogs, hamburgers, BLTs, spaghetti, colas, and chocolate and vanilla ice cream, but no pizza. So David and I order hamburgers. Mom and Gramps have BLTs. We all have colas. Fast food is a rare treat, as Mom usually doesn't approve. But today is certainly a different kind of day for all of us, and Mom says not a word.

"Did you find employment?" David asks.

"First you must tell us about Elvis," Gramps says.

So, between the two of us, we recount the tale of Elvis Presley's street show, and what followed, pausing only when the waitress comes to bring our food. She, like Amanda Harp, seems overjoyed with her job and can't do enough for us.

"That's truly a bizarre story," Mom says when we have finished. "Did he actually say 'gross uniqueness' without smiling?"

"He was serious," I say.

She and Gramps give each other a look.

"Maybe we're being taken in by one of those hidden-camera TV shows," Mom says.

"So, did you find a job?" I ask.

"Yes, factory jobs," Gramps says. "Both of us."

"Factory jobs?" David and I speak at the same time.

"What kind of factory?" I ask.

"Clothing. We'll be notified when to report for learning the sewing machines."

"You're going to make clothes?" I've always loved fashion. It's something Kitty and I had in common. When we were together, we never failed to notice and comment on what people were wearing.

"It appears to be so," Gramps responds. "Apparently Fashion City derives its name from the clothing factory, which is the chief industry here."

"Well, I certainly hope you'll make trendier clothes in that factory than I've seen so far in this place!" I say. "Except for Elvis, everybody's wardrobe has been bor-or-ing. No bright colors. They have no sense of style whatsoever."

I don't mind when Mom, Gramps, and David chuckle at me, because it's good to hear them laugh.

"I think we'll have little choice in the matter," Mom says. "We'll sew what we're given to sew."

"But you're teachers!" David exclaims.

"Yeah, don't they need teachers?" I ask.

"It seems the Fathers have all the teaching jobs sewn up tight," Gramps says. "No pun intended."

"There are no schools as we know them," Mom says. "They teach with computers and television sets. We're to take you and Meggie to the education center tomorrow for placement tests. After that you'll receive instructions via TV. The televisions are already in the apartments."

My eyes meet David's, and I can see my own disappointment reflected there. We have both always enjoyed school. How will we meet other kids?

"Who are these Fathers?" I finally ask.

"Good question," Gramps says. "I'm afraid to ask. I think it must be something everybody on the planet is expected to know."

"And what planet are we on anyway?" David directs his question to Mom, the astronomy professor. "You should know."

"I think Gramps was right—the Carriage has brought us to a parallel universe," Mom says very quietly. "I believe this Earth started out exactly like the one we left behind. But somewhere along the way, they took slightly different turns, which naturally would lead to more different turns. It's impossible to say what all the differences are."

"The butterfly effect," Gramps says.

"The what?" I ask.

"The butterfly effect is best described in a short story by Ray Bradbury about a man who goes into the past and kills a butterfly. As a result, history is changed."

"So you're saying," David interjects, "that even one small deviation on this planet from the other Earth's evolution would have affected many other things?"

"That's correct," Mom says. "The changes would have snowballed and morphed into more changes."

"How do you know it's Earth?" I ask.

Gramps laughs. "Because the man at the employment agency asked us, 'Where on earth did you people come from?'"

"It must be the 1950s on this Earth," I say. "How else could Elvis be so young?"

"That's right," David agrees. "That would also explain why everything seems old-fashioned. Do you think we've gone back in time?"

"No," Gramps says. "The Carriage is not programmed to do that. Unless . . ."

"Unless what?" David prods.

"Unless we hit a time warp somewhere on the way here, but I think if that had happened, we would have felt some kind of turbulence."

"Besides, people here use computers," Mom reminds us.

"That's true," Gramps says. "But let's not ask anybody what year it is. A question like that is sure to turn heads."

After eating lunch, we go to the bus stop and study the map.

"Here's Sector B," Mom says as she points to a spot outside the main business district of the city. "In the residential area. And the bus we need runs every half hour."

Mom buys bus tokens with some of the coupons Amanda Harp gave us. Once en route, David and I watch the city roll by our window. At Fashion City Park, which is at the fringe of the business district, we can see families enjoying the warm day, with children on the playground equipment, picnics spread on the wooden tables, a footrace under way near the entrance.

After the park come blocks and blocks of housing

projects, in which all the buildings are very much alike. They are made from some dark brown material, maybe wood, many stories high, and showing wear and tear.

Each apartment has its own tiny balcony, which gives us hints of what kind of people live inside. Bicycles are stored on some of them. Others are littered with toys or exercise equipment, small grills, lots of potted plants, chairs. The buildings cast shadows over the paved parking lots and sidewalks below. There are few trees.

"Except for the park, I haven't seen a playground, or even a yard," I whisper to David, "and definitely no gardens."

"No sports arenas or baseball fields, not even a vacant lot," he whispers back.

A wave of homesickness washes over me. I wonder what will be said about us when school starts again in the little town we left behind. There probably will be no end to the gossip about us, about the Carriage, about our vanishing into a cloud of vapor. We'll be forgotten as the people we are, and remembered only as "the aliens." Kitty Singer will find a new best friend, and the old Fischer place will be sold to the highest bidder—that is, if they can find someone who is not too freaked out to live where "the aliens" lived. Our garden, our screened porch, our big old breezy kitchen, all could fall into the hands of some family who will never appreciate them like we did.

The bus lurches to a stop and the driver calls out, "Sector B!"

We get off the bus and go to look at our new home.

· 10 ·

The superintendent of Building 9, with keys in hand, is ready to show us to our apartment. He received a call from Amanda Harp telling him to expect us.

"You can call me Tom," he says as we ride the elevator up to the sixth floor. "And I already know your names."

When we don't respond, he goes on to say, "Amanda Harp has told everybody about you. She's got a big mouth, that one. In the housing authority we like to say there are three methods of communication—telephone, television, and tell Amanda."

We laugh politely.

Tom is tall and lanky, all angles and bones. And he has the longest nose and the deepest-set eyes I've ever seen. I can't help staring at him. Mom nudges me to remind me that I'm being rude.

Tom, on the other hand, doesn't mind at all being

rude. He wraps his long arms around his body and leans against the wall, watching us. On the sixth floor we follow him down a hallway to number 603, where he unlocks the door, then hands four keys to Mom.

"You'll like Fashion City," he says. "Everybody does." And he leaves us alone.

In the apartment we find nothing unusual except for a large-screen television set built into one wall of each room, even the bathrooms. Every room is clean, bland, and barely furnished, but I guess it'll do. There is beige linoleum in the kitchen and bathrooms, but the other floors are covered with sturdy carpet, as brown as coffee. The cabinets and Sheetrock are an almond color.

Mom and I take the master bedroom and bathroom. Gramps and David take the smaller two bedrooms with a bathroom between them, where there's a washer and dryer.

The kitchen is the nicest room, as it seems to have been recently renovated. There is plenty of counter and cabinet space, and a small table with four chairs, an electric stove, a microwave, a refrigerator, a dishwasher, and a double sink with garbage disposal.

The main room has two mushroom-colored couches, two matching overstuffed armchairs, a coffee table, and a couple of end tables. Leading off this room are sliding glass doors, through which we can see our small balcony. Together we go out there and stand for a time, looking at this strange city. So muted, so lackluster, so shadowy. And even though the people are of different ethnic backgrounds, somehow they all seem the same.

"We need to think about food for dinner and for breakfast tomorrow," Mom says wearily, interrupting my thoughts. "Shall we go for groceries?"

David and I do not particularly want to go grocery shopping, but Mom and Gramps insist. They say we are needed to help carry the sacks back home, but I know in my heart they are nervous about leaving us alone in this new place. So we stash the backpack in Mom's and my closet, lock up our apartment, and leave again.

In the hallway we come across a woman about Mom's age who seems agitated. With knitted brow, she paces back and forth, mumbling to herself.

We watch her briefly before Mom says, "Can we help you?"

"Maybe you can, yes, maybe so," she says. "You see, I don't know whether I should take the stairs or the elevator."

And she looks at us hopefully, like we might have the answer for her.

"I know the stairs are the best exercise, but I'm going to be late for my dentist appointment," she goes on nervously. It seems like she might burst into tears.

"You're going to be late anyway if you don't do one or the other," Gramps says.

"Oh, you're right, you're right," she says in great agitation. She begins to wring her hands together.

"Then take the elevator, dear," Mom says gently.

"But the stairs are the best exercise," the woman repeats. "What should I do? What *should* I do?"

"Then take the stairs," Gramps suggests.

"But it takes longer to get down," she says, then continues to pace and stew.

From a nearby stairwell, a very pretty girl emerges. No more than twelve or thirteen, she has a face like a flower; her hair is long, dark, and shiny, her eyes a rich brown. Seeing the pacing woman, the girl walks quickly to her.

"Come, Bonnie, what's the problem? I'll help you decide."

Bonnie repeats her dilemma to the young girl.

"You must take the elevator," the girl says firmly. "This one time it's all right. The Fathers would approve."

At the same time she steers the woman toward the elevator. She pushes the Down button and stands whispering soothingly to Bonnie while they wait.

"Are you sure it's the right decision?" Bonnie says when the elevator arrives.

"I'm positive," the young girl says, and guides Bonnie inside.

"Thank you, Jennifer, thank you!" Bonnie cries as the elevator closes behind her.

"Jennifer," David whispers.

I glance at his face. Uh-oh. Is he smitten, or what?

Jennifer turns to us and smiles warmly, saying, "Bonnie lives in the apartment next to yours, number 605. She's a sweet lady and a good neighbor, but she's been rehabilitated so many times, she has no decision-making ability left. She has an advanced case of gross vacillation."

"Gross vacillation?" Mom repeats.

"Yes, it's a common disorder here. It's similar to gross reiteration, also common."

"And that means?"

"Just what it sounds like. A person with gross reiteration repeats the same words and phrases over and over. They get stuck and can't get loose."

"Well, that one I get," Gramps says. "I mean, I can see why."

"And exactly what was Bonnie rehabilitated *for?*" Mom asks.

"One thing and another," Jennifer says. "Mostly war protests. She had three brothers killed in the war."

"What war?" Mom asks.

Jennifer shrugs. "One of the wars against the Fathers."

Then she stretches out a hand to Mom and introduces herself. "I'm Jennifer Gilmore. I live upstairs with my dad and my brother, Colin."

I wonder where her mom is, but don't ask. Mom starts introductions, but Jennifer interrupts.

"I know who you are," she says. "Tom's told everybody about you."

"It's very nice to meet you, Jennifer," Mom is saying. "Do come visit with us when you get a chance, and bring your family."

"Oh, I'd love that!" Jennifer says. "I'll ask Dad."

David watches her as she turns and disappears into the stairwell, where apparently she was on her way down, or up.

"Gross vacillation?" Gramps mutters as we push the elevator button. "Gross reiteration?"

"They do like that word, *gross*, don't they?" I say.

"Jennifer is *not* gross," David says to nobody in particular.

From Tom we get·directions to the nearest grocery store, and find it's in easy walking distance. Sector B Groceries is a small store, very different from the supermarkets we're accustomed to, but larger than a convenience store. It's logically divided into fresh produce, dairy, frozen foods, and then everything else.

The frozen foods take up most of the store. There we find prepared meals of all kinds and sizes, ready to be nuked. Mom has a concerned look on her face. She doesn't like processed food.

"Too much salt and fat," I've heard her say many times. "And too many preservatives. There's no telling what might be in a frozen dinner. You can't even pronounce the ingredients."

But it seems we have no choice at the moment. After selecting our frozen meals and other necessities, vinegar among them, we go to the checkout. Our cashier is a dark-haired young woman whose name tag tells us she is Tammy. She calls out each item as she rings it up on her register. She pops her gum, just like Kitty.

Lining each side of the checkout lane are stacks and stacks of small blue boxes. *LOTUS* is written in white letters on the sides. But something else is missing. What could it be? Here are the candy bars and the batteries and film, but . . . Oh, right! No tabloid newspapers screaming about drunken celebrities and two-headed pigs. It's kinda nice not seeing them. But there are no magazines and newspapers of *any* kind. Come to think of it, I haven't seen any at all in Fashion City.

"Anything else, dear?" Tammy says sweetly to Mom.

"Do you have a newspaper back there?" I jump in, thinking they might be on the floor in bundles behind the counter. I've known this to happen sometimes in busy stores when the help hasn't had time to rack them.

"A n-newspaper!" Tammy sputters. "I should say not! These kids today!" Then she shakes her head, seeming at a loss for further words.

Surprised by her reaction, I say, "What do you mean?"

"For your information, this is not a black-market store!" she spits out with disgust.

"What's a black-market store?" I ask, sincerely eager to know.

But Tammy refuses to answer me. She has pursed her lips and folded her arms across her chest in a holier-than-thou stance.

"If you please, miss," Mom says, refereeing for me, "we have just arrived this day from the Western Province. We are rather uninformed."

The cashier's expression and attitude change immediately. "Ohhhhh." She says the word long and low, making a tall O with her lips. "From the Western Province?" She looks all of us up and down curiously. Then she takes the food rations from Gramps, hands the receipt and some change to Mom, and pats me on the head.

"That's okay, little girl," she says as if I'm five instead of eleven. "How could you know that newspapers were banned after the insurrection?"

"What insurrection?" are the words about to spill out of me, but I catch them just in time, which is probably a good thing.

"Newspapers are a source of discontent," Tammy informs us. "What a blessing for us that they were banned."

"And who, might I ask, banned them?" Gramps says with a fake smile.

"The Fathers, of course!" Tammy answers Gramps's question with a great warm smile of her own. "Praise the Fathers!"

"Indeed, praise the Fathers!" Gramps agrees cynically, but Tammy doesn't get it.

"I know you'll like Fashion City," Tammy says. "Everybody does."

"So we've been told." Gramps keeps up his charade.

We are turning to leave when Tammy calls out suddenly, "Oh, you forgot your Lotus! You're allowed four boxes, one for each of you."

Tammy shoves the Lotus boxes into a plastic bag and hands it to David.

"How much?" Gramps says, digging for the food stamps in his shirt pocket.

"Absolutely free!" Tammy gushes. "A gift to the people from the Fathers."

· 11 ·

"Check the coins!" David says to Mom when we are out on the street. "See what's printed on them!"

"Good idea!" Mom says as she digs around in her jeans pocket for the coins Tammy gave her.

Eagerly we all crowd around Mom to see what's on the nickel, two dimes, and one quarter. All are stamped FASHION CITY, PRAISE THE FATHERS. No date, no country. So we are still in the dark.

"Blue, Mom, blue," David says suddenly. He means that he has spotted a blue streak in Mom's hair.

Mom touches her bare head. "We can't apply the vinegar here."

"Take Meggie's cap," David says as he snatches it from my head. "She doesn't need it. Do you, Meg?" And he laughs like he thinks he's totally funny.

Back in our apartment we go to our rooms and rest, so

that it's well into evening when Gramps and Mom begin preparing our salad for dinner.

David and I sit down in the living room, where we discover that only a few channels are available to us on TV. We watch a brainless sitcom about a family with eight children whose parents work in a clothing factory. Just like in the sitcoms we've become accustomed to on our Earth, everybody is cute and witty and sharp. But talk about your Goody Two-shoes—these kids make me and David look like crooks. They never have to be told twice to do something, and they always say "Praise the Fathers" for every good thing that comes to them. More than once, David and I make like we're barfing.

"Do you think the kids here are like that?" I say to my brother.

"Jennifer doesn't seem that way," he responds. Then, cupping a hand over his mouth, he whispers, "Perfection *sucks*."

Mom hates that word. In fact, her face changes color when she hears it. And here's my geeky brother trying it on for size.

So I encourage him. "You go, David."

By the time we finish dinner and clean up the kitchen, the evening light is gone. Now we are unusually quiet and thoughtful. I know my family is thinking of the old Fischer place, as I am, and what we might have been doing at this hour if we'd been lucky enough to stay there. We slump heavily on the living room furniture. Gramps picks up the remote control and clicks the TV on again.

"Maybe we can get some news," he says.

A Lotus commercial is playing. The words are the same as the ones we saw on the billboards this morning, but set to music.

Take it for a headache or a heartache.
Just one Lotus
For a difference you will notice.
Lotus! Lotus! Lotus!

"I wonder what that stuff is," Mom says.

"Some kind of tranquilizer, is my guess," Gramps says. "I had the feeling that many of the people we saw today were *on* something."

"No kidding?" David says. "That would explain their unmitigated joy."

"*On* something, for real?" I say.

Mom goes into the kitchen and brings out a box of Lotus. She opens it up and pulls out two handfuls of blue pills, each one wrapped in hard clear plastic.

"No literature," Mom says, looking inside the empty box. "Nothing to tell us what the ingredients are."

"Remember the story of Ulysses?" Gramps says.

We nod. We read it together at the old Fischer place.

"Remember the land of the lotus eaters?"

"Vaguely," Mom says. "Refresh our memory."

"The people who lived there ate of the lotus plant and lost all ambition. After his crew tasted it, Ulysses had to force them back onto the ship because they had no desire to return home."

Mom stuffs the pills back into the box. "We will not be swallowing any of these."

A series of slogans begins rolling across the TV screen while the silky-smooth voice of a woman reads the words. Tranquil music plays softly in the background.

Stay healthy and alive for Vacation 65!
Conformity is security.
Conformity is contentment.
The daydreamer is discontented.
I will gladly give four years to serve the Fathers.
Everybody likes Fashion City.
Conformity is security.
Conformity is contentment.
Praise the Fathers!

The music is soothing, hypnotic, and without the help of Lotus or anything else, we are lulled into a weird kind of spell. The doorbell startles us back to reality.

Gramps opens the door to reveal Tom standing there with a clipboard in his hand. His Adam's apple bobs comically in his long, thin neck as he yells importantly, "Eight-thirty curfew! Let me see your faces."

The four of us are right in front of him, but he counts heads out loud as if there are a dozen of us in the room.

"One . . . two . . . three . . . four, all accounted for," he says. "Lockdown! You can't go out again until six a.m."

And he leaves us mystified. Our door makes a clicking sound.

Gramps tries the knob. It doesn't budge. "Lockdown?" he screeches. "This is outrageous!"

"So we aren't allowed outside from eight-thirty at night until six in the morning?" David says.

"Are we in prison?" I say.

Mom's face has gone scarlet, as it's prone to do when she's upset. She starts to say something, but is interrupted when every television in our apartment—seven, to be exact—comes on. Gramps grabs the remote and begins punching buttons angrily. No luck. He lurches from room to room, trying to turn off or turn down the TVs. Nothing works.

"Welcome to *The Family Hour*," comes the same warm female voice we heard earlier. "An hour of entertainment for the entire family, brought to you by the Fathers."

· 12 ·

Being hungry for information, and learning that the first item on *The Family Hour* is news, we sit down again on the mushroom-colored furniture. There is no choice about listening. Gramps closes all the bedroom and bathroom doors to cut down the noise, but the volume simply can't be controlled. It seems to be set for the hard of hearing.

"Good evening," the young announcer is saying. She is pretty in spite of her dull gray suit. "I'm Sherry Cross, and our first report is from the Fashion City Police Department. We regret to inform you of three arrests today."

There appears a mug shot of a man who looks like he's so mad, he could chew you up and spit you out.

"Forty-three-year-old Harley Meeks of Sector C was arrested for leaving work and going to Fashion City Park without permission," the announcer says. She is clearly tickled, as Kitty would say. "We all know it is not Sector C's turn for the park, but Mr. Meeks pleaded confusion." The announcer chuckles. "The judge ordered him to forgo his next two holidays."

There appears a mug shot of a teenage girl who is obviously in a state of shock.

"Sixteen-year-old Ginger Shore of Sector D was arrested for evading the military police for fourteen days. She was sentenced to an extra season of duty."

We all cut our eyes at each other. Sixteen years old? Military police?

A mug shot of Elvis appears.

"Twenty-one-year-old Elvis Presley of Sector E was arrested for breaking the conformity laws with his street show. According to the arresting officer, Presley's hair and sideburns were too long, his clothing too appealing, and his performance too tantalizing. He was charged with three counts of gross uniqueness and sentenced to seven days of rehabilitation for each count.

"In other news, a new family arrived in Fashion City today. Having escaped from the Western Province, Mr. Sam Lane; his daughter, Linda Blue; and Mrs. Blue's two children, David and Meggie, walked all the way with very little food and water, traveling mostly in the dark, and retiring to the undergrowth during daylight."

We all sit erect and look at Sherry Cross with startled expressions.

"They were found by a police officer this morning, sleeping in the park," she continues.

And there we are on television—Mom, Gramps, David, and I—walking down the street from the employment agency, looking for a place to eat, and probably talking about Elvis, though our conversation is not audible.

"Where was the camera?" I wonder out loud. Nobody answers.

Sherry Cross goes on, "Mrs. Blue told this reporter, 'It was all for freedom, and we would go through the same ordeal again in order to escape the gross tyranny and oppression in the Western Province.'

"Mrs. Blue's own husband, the father of her children, was murdered by the Lincoln-King regime."

"Wh-what!" I sputter.

"The nerve!" Mom gasps.

"I asked Mrs. Blue if all the stories we've been hearing about that place are really true, and, my dear fellow citizens, I must regretfully report that they are! According to the Blues, people really are starving to death in the Western Province. They have been reduced to"—the announcer halts for a moment to shudder, and places a small white hand over her heart—"to eating rats . . . and . . . even resorting to cannibalism." She finishes in a shaky voice.

Then, collecting herself instantly, Sherry Cross smiles brightly for the camera and takes up the story again in a cheerful voice. "The Blues have been given a three-bedroom in Sector B, where they will recover from their ordeal before going to work in the factory. Welcome, Mr. Lane, Mrs. Blue, Meggie, and David. We know you'll like Fashion City. Everybody does."

We are too amazed even to comment to each other. The news continues with a video of the big white bus with VACATION 65 in purple on the side.

"As everybody must know by now, it's Vacation 65 time again. It seems the last one was only yesterday, instead of last season. Today twenty-seven of our beloved seniors, upon reaching the age of sixty-five, found it was finally their turn to ride the white bus."

There follows a tape of Sherry Cross interviewing several old people before they boarded the bus earlier in the day. They are all laughing and hugging each other, and talking about the goodness of the Fathers.

"And what is your name, sweetheart?" Sherry asks one of the ladies.

"Well, it's not Sweetheart!" the old woman retorts. She's giddy with excitement.

"Excu-uu-se me!" Sherry Cross says with a laugh.

"My name is Anna Mary Robertson Moses."

"And in what capacity did you serve?" Sherry asks.

"I worked at the factory. I started there at the age of twenty," Anna Mary says. "Then I married and raised ten children, but continued working until it was time for Vacation 65."

"Ten children!" Sherry exclaims with exaggerated astonishment. "How delightful! You have given ten children to serve the Fathers. What a well-deserved vacation!"

"But it won't be all play. Oh, no. This will be a working vacation!" Anna Mary says proudly. "I plan to paint pictures. It's something I've always wanted to do. And now I will have time."

"Grandma Moses!" Gramps says with a gasp. "That's who she is!"

"Who's Grandma Moses?" I ask.

"Tell you later," he mumbles, too intent on the screen to explain right now.

Then the show returns to Sherry Cross back in the studio. "Wait a moment . . . Just one moment," she says as she touches her earpiece. A big smile is on her face. "We have live pictures coming in at this very second . . . pictures of the lucky seniors arriving in Farlands for Vacation 65."

There is the same bunch of old people getting off an airport van, including the man David and I saw saying goodbye to his family. Clutching a box of Lotus under one arm, he seems bewildered but happy. Grandma Moses seems unaware of the camera, so intent is she on gazing at her surroundings. Vacation 65 is located on a beach with sand as white as sugar. It's the most beautiful resort one could imagine.

Each senior is welcomed by a perky young guide with a frothy tropical drink in her hands. After accepting the drinks, the old people are escorted toward the grand hotel on the oceanfront.

Then the scene cuts away to still shots of the area—a waterfall, a garden filled with exotic flowers, gazebos, a golf course, a cruise ship, an indoor-outdoor swimming pool, a gurgling creek meandering through a stretch of woods, with petite and picturesque bridges, and hammocks stretched between the trees.

"What a great place to paint!" Gramps says. "I'd love a vacation like that."

"I think you have to be sixty-five," David says with a grin, "and we all know *you* are only sixty!"

Gramps grins too, and tosses a pillow at David.

Last, but far from least, there's a state-of-the-art hospital where smiling doctors and nurses stand poised to give the best medical care available to these lucky seniors, it is announced, with no expense spared.

After leaving the happy Vacation 65 group, *The Family Hour* camera focuses on a grumpy man in a brown suit who gives us a sermon regarding water waste in Fashion City. There has been too much of it, he says, and the Fathers are not pleased. The people are reminded to refrain from washing clothes or dishes unless there is a full load, to limit showers to five minutes, and to be more frugal in flushing.

"Remember our motto: 'If it's yellow, let it mellow, but if it's brown, flush it down!'"

David and I burst into laughter at this sudden humor from the crabby announcer, but there isn't a hint of a smile on his face.

Then he announces that the consumption of electricity has risen almost five percent in the last year, and suggestions are given for cutting back on precious energy.

"Don't burn lights during the day!" he says sternly. "And when you're not loaded down with consumer goods, take the stairs instead of the elevator! Don't be so soft. Remember the sacrifices of the Fathers, and make a few of your own!"

There follows on *The Family Hour* an emotional pep rally for the Fathers. It's creepy to watch the ceremonies involving people of all ages, and listen to the sounds from other apartments in our building. Hallelujahs and screeching praises are bouncing off the walls. In fact, our neighbors sound like a football crowd. One thing is sure—in Fashion City everybody luuuves the Fathers.

Following the pep rally, a group of young people in white robes and glowing faces sings praises to the Fathers in sweet clear voices.

Praise the Fathers, for they are good . . .
The Fathers take care of the people . . .

These themes are repeated in many ways. And then the same mantras we saw earlier roll across the screen as Sherry Cross reads them aloud to us and soft music plays in the background. It's hypnotic.

I will gladly give four years to serve the Fathers.
For the Fathers are good.

Finally the hour comes to an end. Sherry Cross informs her audience we have thirty minutes to prepare for bed, at which time all lights in the city will be extinguished.

"Lockdown and lights-out," Gramps mutters between clenched teeth.

Mom's face is troubled, but she speaks calmly. "While in residence here, we shall follow the rules."

"Do we have a choice?" Gramps says.

We say good night and go to our bedrooms. After brushing my teeth, I change for bed, and remember the last time I put on these same pajamas. It was at the old Fischer place in my own sky-blue room just off the upstairs porch. That was only last night! But it seems like days ago and worlds away. . . . Well, it *was* worlds away.

"I feel like Alice," Mom says when we are lying side by side in bed, "and I've just fallen down the rabbit hole."

"Or we're in the land of Oz," I say dreamily, remembering David's remark about not being in Kansas anymore. "Maybe the wizard will help us."

Then I can say no more, because my mind is whirling with fantastic visions.

The angry eyes of the mob chasing us from our home on Earth . . . Elvis Presley singing for coins in the street . . . a white bus taking old people on vacation . . . a transparent rocket tearing through space . . . a burly cop scolding David . . . the Log recording our memories of Earth . . . fanatical voices screeching in praise of the Fathers.

Finally my mind shuts down, and I sleep.

· 13 ·

It's very dark when I wake up to find myself alone. Softly I call for Mom, but I get no answer. I sit straight up in bed. What if my family has flown away in the Carriage and left me behind in this loopy world?

Near panic, I call more loudly, "Mom!" No answer.

I'm close to tears as I slip out of bed and try to snap on the lamp. It doesn't work. Neither does the wall switch. In this place, when they say lights-out, they really mean it. I tiptoe into the dark hallway, and take only a few steps before I run into somebody.

"It's just me," Gramps says.

My eyes overflow as I go into his arms. "I woke up alone," I say, and he hugs me.

"We would never leave you, Meggie B."

Of course they wouldn't. I am such a baby. I wipe my

tears on Gramps's shirt. I don't want David to see me like this.

"Your mom just went out to get some fresh air, and found me and David on the balcony," Gramps explains. "Since that door isn't locked, we're assuming it's okay to be out there. Mom asked me to come and get you, for it has rained."

We find Mom and David huddled together on a blanket. Mom has spread a shower curtain under the blanket to keep it dry. She stretches out her arms for me, and I crawl into them.

"Smell the rain?" she says.

It's a fairly fresh smell, but mixed up with gas fumes and asphalt, it can't compare with the summer rains in North Carolina.

Gramps snuggles on the other side of me, and I feel safe again. We settle against the wall and listen to the silence. The people of Fashion City are asleep behind their locked doors. What do they dream of?

In my mind I am singing *"Near the village, the peaceful village, the lion sleeps tonight"*—when suddenly the sound of real singing reaches my ears. It's a man's voice coming from the balcony directly above ours. He accompanies himself on the guitar. We barely breathe as we listen.

I remember moonless nights across the frozen land.
Soft flakes of snow were falling.
Freedom in the wilderness back when the earth was new.
Traps and guns were faraway and few.

I remember cold blue nights of ice and wind,
Moving softly 'neath the silver pines.
How those haunting mem'ries call me,
Saying once the wolves were here.
Wild hearts without fear!

"What a lovely voice," Mom whispers in the darkness.

"It's extraordinary," Gramps says softly. "He seems to be singing from the wolf's point of view. And such a melancholy song. I can almost hear them howling."

"I'm reminded of your father," Mom says sadly to me and David. "He had an amazing voice. Do you remember how he used to come into your room at night and sing you to sleep?"

"I do," David says. "Our beds were suspended from the ceiling."

"I remember too," I say, surprising myself. "Our house was round and silver, and it sat high on a cliff." So that dream I had—it must have been a real memory. Has it been in my head all these years?

"And there were clouds all around us," David adds.

"They were clouds of pollution!" Gramps says with a wry laugh. "But when I was a small boy, the air was clear enough that you could see blue hills in the distance."

"I remember having to wear protective face gear when we went outside," David says with a sigh. "But Dad got sick anyway."

"Many people did," Mom says. "And when your father was near the end, he made me promise to take our children to a safe place."

She hasn't talked about Dad for a long time, and we haven't asked about him, because we know it makes her sad.

"And I did promise. But now? I simply don't know how safe this place is."

The night breeze picks up Mom's words and carries them away. I look out upon this strange still city. The streets are wet and full of reflections. The air is thick with shadows and haze. There is no moon, and there are no stars.

"What kind of people don't have pets?" Mom whispers.

It's true we have not seen or heard a dog or cat or any other kind of pet. We've seen pigeons flying around, and a few other birds, and that seems to be the extent of animal life here. Maybe there are squirrels in the park. I'm awfully glad we didn't adopt a golden retriever. It would have been heartbreaking to leave it behind, but impossible to keep it in Fashion City.

"Do we want to stay here or move on to another world right away?" Mom asks us.

"How long does it take to set up the Carriage?" I say.

"First we have to fit the dowels into their sockets," Mom says. "That takes only thirty minutes or so. The dowels act as pumps to restore the walls, and that takes about twenty-four hours."

"We can set it up in the morning if you want," Gramps says.

"Let's give Fashion City a little more time," David says, and somehow I know he is thinking of Jennifer.

"Perhaps we should," Mom says. "In the meantime, Gramps and I will learn more about operating the Carriage, and we'll search the computer for a good place to land."

On the balcony above us two younger voices have joined the first one in harmony.

How those haunting mem'ries call me,
Saying once the wolves were here.
Wild hearts without fear!

· 14 ·

"You'll like it here. Everybody does."

These words are turning themselves over and over in my brain at six a.m. when all the television sets come on again. A male voice rouses us from our sleep.

"Time for exercise, happy people of Fashion City. Hit the floor. One! Two!"

I peep out from under the covers. A man is doing jumping jacks.

"The Fathers want you to have strong bodies. Three! Four! A strong body serves far better than a weak one. Five! Six!"

There's no going back to sleep now. Mom and I watch the man exercising for a few moments before she says, "Well, we do need to keep in shape."

With those words she crawls out of bed and hits the

floor as the man suggests. I watch her exercising for a time before I join her.

"So, who is Grandma Moses?" I remember to ask Gramps at breakfast.

"On our Earth she was a famous American painter," Gramps says, "but she didn't start painting until she was old—in her seventies, maybe. She taught herself, and she was remarkably talented. Most of her life was spent taking care of a family. She raised ten children, and it was only when she was old that she had time to do her own thing."

"Hey, I know what we can do," David says. "We'll set Gramps up as a fortune-teller. When Grandma Moses comes back from vacation, Gramps can look at her palm and tell her she's going to be a rich and famous artist."

"And he can tell Elvis Presley he's going to be a rich and famous performer," I say. "There must be other Earth doubles here too!"

Mom is smiling at us. "Yes," she says, "I'm quite sure of it. And I'm so glad to see we're all in a better mood after sleeping."

The doorbell interrupts our conversation, and Gramps goes to see who's there.

"Telephone installation service!" a man's voice says cheerfully.

"We didn't order a telephone," Gramps tells him.

"It's standard procedure," the man explains. "Everybody gets a phone. If you don't want to use it, fine, but it's required."

"Do let him in," Mom calls out. "You never know when we'll have an emergency."

Gramps and the man come into the kitchen. With his back to us, the man begins installing an old-fashioned black phone with a curly cord on the wall. As we continue eating, we can't carry on a normal conversation because we are self-conscious with him in the room. But the man is all smiles and warmth and tries to put us at ease.

"Call me Joe," he says.

"Okay, Joe," Gramps agrees.

We are about to drift back into silence again, with the only sound being the clinking of utensils against plates, when Joe says, "So you folks escaped the Western Province?"

When nobody answers right away, he turns around to look at us. Mom simply nods.

"How are them scalawags doing now that things are going bad for them?" he asks.

"Who?" we all say at the same time.

"You know, Lincoln and King!" Joe goes on. "They promised the people that things would be better for them if they got away from the Fathers. And now look at 'em, eating rats and all! Bet they're not so full of promises these days, huh?"

"Right," Mom says weakly.

Joe laughs long and loud.

"What do you know about Lincoln and King?" Gramps inquires.

"Not much," Joe replies. "I was only a bit of a boy, but

I do remember the night of the insurrection when the people broke down the police barriers. There were just too many of them. The police couldn't hold 'em back. For a kid like me, it was real scary."

We wait, hoping he'll say more, and we are not disappointed.

"How's old Abe doing these days?"

"Whooo?" Mom says cautiously.

"Abe . . . You know, Abraham Lincoln, the instigator. I know he's old, but he's still alive and kicking over there, ain't he?"

I drop my fork. Abraham Lincoln is the Lincoln in the Lincoln-King regime?

"Oh . . . oh, yes, he's still at it," Mom says. "Do you remember him well?"

"Not well, but we lived in the same sector, and I heard he was a pretty good boy till he got tangled up with Martin Luther King, Jr.!"

Now all our mouths fall open and our eyes meet, as we put two and two together. Martin Luther King, Jr., is the other half of the Lincoln-King regime?

"Together they got in trouble more than anybody. Couldn't stay out of jail."

"J-jail?" I sputter. "For what?"

"First of all, for even hanging out together. It wasn't allowed. Also for growing a beard, for staying out late, for trying to integrate the factory, for organizing a union . . . You name it. They both went through rehabilitation more times than you could shake a stick at, but it made no difference. They just couldn't conform."

"Would you call them grossly unique?" I say.

"Grossly unique, and grossly unpatriotic!" Joe says. "You should ask Tom about Abe. They were boys together."

"Our building supervisor?" Gramps asks.

"That's him, Tom Lincoln. Him and Abe are brothers."

So that explains Tom's appearance, all the angles and bones.

"But he's not a thing like Abe," Joe continues. "He was one of the first to swear allegiance to the Fathers after the insurrection."

"I have lost track of time," Mom says. "I'm so forgetful sometimes. How many years ago was that, anyway?"

"Derned if I know," Joe says. "Who keeps up with years anymore? Not the folks of Fashion City. The Fathers do that for us."

"How so?" Gramps asks.

"Oh, they send out reminders on important days, like when it's your turn to use the park, when it's time to get drafted at sixteen, and when you're old enough for Vacation 65. Otherwise, we don't need to know what day it is, or what year either."

So that answers the question of the calendar. Nobody cares what year it is.

"Oh, we know what season it is," Joe says. "That's the important thing. We do everything by season—group birthdays, for example."

"Group birthdays?" I ask.

"Yeah, you know your sector gets to go to the park

once each season. So if you was born in the spring, then you could celebrate the spring birthday party in the park when it's time for your sector to go."

Group birthdays? How special is *that*?

"But you, sir." Joe turns to Gramps. "You certainly must remember the insurrection! Better than any of us, I'm sure."

"Well . . ." Gramps doesn't know what to say. "Sorta."

"That's not a thing you're likely to forget," Joe persists.

"Not unless you get hit on the head and lose your memory," Gramps says.

Startled, Mom, David, and I look at him, and he winks. "I have suffered from amnesia ever since."

"Is that right? Don't remember a thing, do you?"

"Very little." Gramps lies easily. "It was a hard blow."

"Well, I reckon you know that Lincoln and King accused the Fathers of being oppressive. They led more than half the people out of Fashion City and established their own regime in the Western Province, which, I don't have to tell you, ain't a fit place to live. Since then our only news of them has come in bits and pieces, mostly through people like you who have managed to escape. You're a lucky bunch, is all I can say."

"And where are these other escapees now?" Mom asks.

"Who knows?" Joe replies. "They get jobs and places to live, like you all did, and next thing you know, they're part of the mix. Not to worry. You'll blend in soon enough. Then you'll forget the past and become just like the rest of us."

Now *that* is a scary thought!

Joe grins at us, like he's pleased with his little pep talk. Then he packs his tools and stands up to leave. "Welcome to Fashion City. You'll like it here. Everybody does."

When he's gone, we sit there looking at each other, trying to make sense of what we've heard.

"Abraham Lincoln and Martin Luther King, Jr., alive at the same time, in the present?" Mom says. "That's a lot to take in."

"There's an evolutionary theory," Gramps says, "that great leaders appear on their respective planets at the time when they are most needed."

"I wrote a paper on Abraham Lincoln in my history class," David says, "and he did have a younger brother by the name of Thomas, but he died as an infant."

"Apparently, on this Earth, he lived," Mom says. "Perhaps because he was born at a time when medical technology was more advanced."

"I wonder if things really are as bad in the Western Province as people say," Gramps says. "I'm inclined to believe it's merely propaganda. After all, look how *The Family Hour* quoted us when they didn't even interview us."

"Is it possible the Western Province is more like America?" David says.

"Entirely possible," Gramps says. "With Abraham Lincoln and Martin Luther King, Jr., in charge, you would expect a civilized place. But who knows?"

"Maybe we could go there," I say.

"Not so fast," Mom says. "We don't know for sure what it's like over there. It could be as bad as they say."

"Yeah, if it's so great," David says, "why would people be coming back here?"

"Good question," Mom says. "Very good question."

· 15 ·

"We can't wear these clothes another day," Mom says after breakfast. "We're beginning to smell. Let's go shopping."

We make a list of things we need, leave Building 9, and hop onto a bus for the Fashion City Mall. It's near the clothing factory where Mom and Gramps are going to work, and we have to cross over a bridge. Gazing down into the murky water is like looking into a giant mud puddle. Things float on top. Green slime laps against the banks. A light wind is blowing dirty foam over the slime. I half expect some hideous ecological beast to rise from the muck. I'll bet there wasn't a nastier river even on Chroma.

At the water's edge several men are working on large white signs with letters in bright blue fluorescent paint. Some of the signs are finished and propped up to dry.

David elbows me and whispers, "Look what the signs say."

NO SWIMMING. NO FISHING. NO WADING.

"What are we—stupid?" David whispers again.

I giggle.

"Even if a person wanted to drown himself," David goes on, "he'd want to find a more sanitary watery grave."

The mall, by American standards, is small. There are only three clothing stores, and all of them sell the same clothes—in white, black, gray, navy, olive, and brown. Many of the T-shirts display the slogans we've heard again and again since coming to Fashion City, the most common one being *Praise the Fathers*.

The other stores are selling things like sewing machines, radios, guitars, bicycles, and toys. The toys are limited to guns and military supplies, dolls and stuffed animals.

We walk into one of the clothing stores, and I'm in the sleepwear section trying in vain to find something I like, when I hear someone muttering.

"Animals are filthy and carry disease. Animals are filthy and carry disease. Animals are filthy and carry disease." And on and on and on.

I peep around a rack of robes and see a display of teddy bears and other stuffed animals tucked in with the pj's. I'm surprised to see that many of the animals are brightly colored. And standing beside the display is Alison Fink, a girl from my fifth-grade class. I always thought she was so cool because she had a fantastic imagination. She made up stories about the people in our class and how she thought we would turn out in the future. In my story, I was to become a famous astronaut. As for Alison, she loved animals, and wrote about herself as a veterinarian.

At the moment she's playing absentmindedly with the stuffed animals as she repeats that dumb phrase.

"Alison! I'm so happy to see you!" But no, no, I have to remind myself, this is not the Alison I used to know. This is her double.

Alison glances up at me but doesn't lose her train of thought. She goes on with her repetitious phrase while she plays with the toys. She is slow and deliberate in saying each word, like she doesn't want to miss a syllable. "Animals are filthy and carry disease. Animals are filthy and carry disease."

So this must be one of those cases of gross reiteration Jennifer mentioned. That phrase is stuck in Alison's head, probably because it's been repeated to her so often, and now she can't get it out. It must be hard for her to live in a world without animals.

I watch and listen for a moment, but it's really nerve-wracking. I'm reminded of how a tune gets stuck in my head sometimes and nearly drives me nuts. What I have to do is replace it with another tune that I like better. Then I concentrate on the tune I like, and hum it out loud, or in my head, and presto! The other tune evaporates.

I move over to stand beside Alison, and pick up a furry cat. "Wouldn't you just love to be an animal doctor?" I say.

"Animals are filthy and carry disease" is her response.

I pick up a big green frog. It looks a bit like Kermit.

"You know," I say, holding the frog in front of her, "I bet it's not easy being green."

She pays me no attention. Obviously, when you have this affliction, you are able to focus on nothing but the words you are reiterating.

"Let's name him Kermit," I say. "If you were to write his story, how would it go?"

This time when she looks at me, there's a flicker in her eyes. But then they go dead again, and she goes back to her browsing and mumbling. "Animals are filthy and carry disease."

"I love animals," I whisper close to her ear.

"Animals are filthy and carry disease."

"In your story, Kermit could be a frog who is very lonely because he's the only green animal. He's unique, but he can't help it. That's just the way he was made."

Now I *know* she's listening. I can tell by her expression. Her voice goes soft.

" 'It's Not Easy Being Green' would make a good title," I tell her.

"Animals are filthy and carry disease."

I hold up the frog again, and say, "Animals are totally wonderful, but it's not easy being green."

Now she pauses and looks at me curiously.

I say "It's not easy being green" again, then again and again. She continues with her own phrase, but I say mine faster and louder. "It's not easy being green."

We go on this way as if we are in competition with

one another, when all of a sudden she derails. "Animals are green and filthy," she says. Now her face is puzzled. "Animals are easy . . . carry green disease."

"It's not easy being green," I say.

"Green is filthy—" she starts, but I interrupt her.

"It's not easy being different."

"It's not easy being me," she responds, and I think she is really trying to carry on a conversation with me. "I mean, I mean . . . it's not easy being green."

"Yes!" Now I'm excited. "It's not easy being green!"

A slow smile comes onto her face. "It's not easy being green!" she repeats. "It's not easy being green!"

"You've read stories, haven't you?" I ask, and I think— but I'm not sure—she nods her head at me. "I know you could write a good one."

"It's not easy being green," she says. "It's not easy being green."

At that moment I see David. He's watching and listening to us, and he's not smiling. I walk over and whisper to him, "Look, David, it's Alison Fink."

"Not really, Meggie." He whispers too. "You shouldn't be saying those things to her."

"Why not?"

"Listen to her. Nobody will understand. They'll think she's nuts."

"Do *you* understand?" I ask him.

He says nothing, just looks at me.

"But don't you see? She's come unstuck," I say. "Look at her face."

Alison picks up the green frog and says to it, "It's not

easy being green." Then she hugs it to her and smiles at me and David. "It's not easy being green."

"I admit she's stuck on something else now," I say, "but at least it's different."

"Alison!" someone calls, and a woman comes around the end of the robes. It's her mom. I've seen her picking Alison up at school.

Alison hands the frog to her mom and points to the cash register. "It's not easy being green," she says.

"What on earth are you saying now?" Mrs. Fink asks, obviously irritated, as she takes the frog and guides her daughter toward the checkout.

"It's not easy being green," Alison says. "It's not easy being green."

"Don't say that out loud!" Mrs. Fink orders.

Alison begins to whisper, and the two of them move out of earshot.

"You've just made things harder for her," David says to me.

"I don't think so," I say hotly. "You don't know everything."

He shrugs and walks away from me.

In another half hour or so, we have settled on two pairs of jeans and four plain T-shirts for each of us, plus socks, pajamas, and underwear for everybody.

Amanda Harp didn't give us enough rations for so much clothing, but "Not to worry," the bubbling store clerk tells us. "You can charge it to the factory, and the costs will be deducted from your paychecks, a little at a time, of course. The Fathers take care of the people here."

"Is that right?" Gramps says, acting like he's really surprised, and he gives the clerk his best I'm-poking-fun-at-you-and-you-don't-even-know-it smile.

"Oh, yes, praise the Fathers," the clerk says as she glances through our purchases. "But . . ."

"But what?" Mom says.

The clerk seems a bit uneasy, but goes on. "Let me suggest that you buy at least one shirt that praises the Fathers. You know, since you're new here, everybody is curious about your loyalty."

"Oh, of course," Mom mumbles. "Good advice."

Gramps says nothing, but tags along with Mom as she goes back to the T-shirt rack. Without enthusiasm, they come back to the register with one shirt for each of us that displays some kind of slogan about the Fathers.

Gramps winks and whispers to me and David, "We don't have to wear them all at the same time, like we're quadruplets. We'll just have one token patriot per day."

Back in our apartment David and I prepare to go to the education center for our placement tests.

"I want you to do something for me," Mom says when we appear in our dull new clothes. She clears her throat nervously. "I know I have always told you to do your best at everything."

We nod. Is she worried about this test?

"Well, today I want you to do just the opposite."

"What!"

"Yes, I want you to do poorly on this test—not too poorly, but aim for what was considered low average in the schools you have attended in the past."

"But why, Mom?" I ask.

"I know why," David says. "They like to think we're from a savage place, as Officer Brent said. So we'll let them think it."

"That's right," Mom says. "If the Fathers—whoever they are—realize how educated and intelligent we are, they'll see us as a threat. It's obvious they like to keep people in the dark about many things, and under their control."

"So we should flunk the test?" I say.

"Yes, for your own good, flunk it."

At the education center a young woman named Amy carefully goes over instructions for use of the computer.

"This is called a mouse," Amy explains, "and this is a keyboard."

David and I have used computers all our lives, but we play dumb, listen carefully, and ask the appropriate questions. Then Amy leaves us alone with the computer test, after we promise to call her if we have any trouble.

David and I have the same test, and it's so easy, I manage to breeze through it in no time flat. Then I go back over it and deliberately mark several answers wrong. I look over at David, who whispers, "Do it again more slowly."

So I go through the test one more time, then check out the computer. That's when I find an icon for an Internet connection. Excitedly I click on it, but nothing happens, so I click again. This time I get a yellow warning triangle: INACCESSIBLE!

Then a message comes up on the screen for me: *Meggie Blue is to be placed in fourth level, channel three, one o'clock*. David's message says he is to be placed in the fifth level, channel four, at one o'clock. So it looks like I've finally managed to beat David at something—I've out-flunked him.

Amy comes back into the room with a box of school supplies for us.

"Tune in to your class tomorrow and follow instructions," she says. "At the end of the season you'll return here for testing again on the computer."

"Meggie's in fourth level and I'm in fifth," David says with disgust as we are walking home with Mom and Gramps. "Do you think that's equivalent to the fourth and fifth grade?"

"I imagine their grade levels are different from what you're used to," Mom says. "What kind of questions did you get?"

"A lot of math," I say. "But it was easy."

"What else?" Gramps asks. "Any history, geography, science?"

He's our token patriot for the day in his ugly gray shirt that reads THE FATHERS TAKE CARE OF THE PEOPLE.

"Just elementary grammar," David says. "Then we had to read some paragraphs and answer questions about what we read."

"I have a feeling the Fathers don't encourage real education," Mom says. "They teach the people only what they need to know in order to live and work in this society."

"I wonder about art and music," Gramps says. "The kids here must be starved for self-expression."

"Maybe you could start some art classes yourself, Gramps," David says.

"I doubt it would be allowed," Gramps says. "Something tells me if the people here get any instruction in the arts, they have to teach themselves."

"There was an Internet connection on my computer," I tell them, "but it was useless. I couldn't get online."

"Well, it's good to know they *have* an Internet," Gramps says, "but I'm guessing only the Fathers have access to it."

"Another way to keep people in the dark," Mom comments.

"Right," Gramps says. "As they say, knowledge is power."

"We don't even have a radio," David says. "Wonder what's on *it?*"

"No doubt the same stuff we get on TV," Mom says. "Who needs more of that?"

I'm sure David won't mention to Mom what happened with Alison Fink in the clothing store. He's not a squealer. And it's for sure I'm not going to tell, because I know Mom would not approve. She would say my getting involved was like violating the Prime Directive on *Star Trek,* meaning you never interfere with the ways of the natives.

· 16 ·

The following afternoon, David and I tune in to our classes at one o'clock while Mom and Gramps go to the grocery store. David uses the TV in the living room and I go into my and Mom's bedroom. I spread out my school supplies on the bed and go to work.

At the end of the period I'm instructed to place my lessons in a pocket that is attached to our front door, where they will be collected by the building superintendent. Then what? I wonder. I'll be free for the rest of the day, but free to do what? We can't play sports. We have nothing to read. I would love to go to the park, but it looks like you can be arrested for going there out of turn. And television is a joke. No Disney channel, no MTV, no Animal Planet, no game shows, no movies, not even real news.

I look around this bare room. It symbolizes all the

drabness of this place. How could you ever have pleasant dreams in a room so starved of color and decoration? Then my eye falls on the closet, and I remember the Carriage. Yeah, it's stashed in there. And it has a computer. If I messed around with that computer, Gramps could actually blow his cool with me, and Mom's face might burst into flames. But if they don't know . . .

I go to the closet and pull the backpack down from the shelf. I rummage around in the Carriage material and find the control panel, which Mom folded so carefully down to the size of a book.

Suddenly there's a tap on my door. "Finished, Meg?" It's David.

"Uh . . . no, I'm still working."

I'm glad my brother has the good manners not to come barging into my bedroom without being asked.

"For real?" he says. "My class is over."

"Mine has a ways to go," I lie.

I climb back into the center of the bed and open the control panel. The computer automatically lights up. The keyboard is built into the panel just below the tiny screen. The mouse is a ball that rolls in the keyboard. A question pops up.

DO YOU WISH TO EXPLORE FAR WORLDS TODAY?

I click on yes.

For the next ten minutes or so I'm totally engrossed as I focus on a distant planet called Crisis, all circled with rainbow rings like Saturn, but it's not Saturn. The text tells me strange and wonderful things about this world.

In spite of the beauty and richness of their planet, the people are constantly embroiled in some kind of battle. The civilization is many millions of years old, but for some reason, its people are like children who never grow up.

I think of the blue streaks I would so like to see in my hair because they are a mark of maturity in the world I came from. I wonder if I can do a search on Chroma. . . . Then it hits me like a truck. *This text is not in English.* It is, of course, written in Chromish. I have been reading Chromish!

I scan the menu. Yes, I can read this. Yes, I understand that. Yes, but how?

A flash of memory comes. I see myself as a three-year-old resting my head on Dad's pillow. I see a diamond-shaped electronic book, and I see my dad's finger move down a column of symbols as he reads aloud to me.

The sound of voices in the living room interrupts my thoughts. Mom and Gramps are back from the store. I scramble to close the control panel, tuck it into the backpack, and return it to the closet shelf.

As Mom and Gramps are preparing dinner, David and I watch another idiotic sitcom, but my mind is racing. I can read Chromish, and I'm almost sure that David can't. I don't think he can even speak it very well anymore. I have all this information at my fingertips in the Carriage computer. What am I going to do with it? I can learn anything, go anywhere—cyberwise, that is.

The doorbell rings, and David leaps to his feet. It's Jennifer with two other people, who must be her brother and father. The boy is a few years older than Jennifer, and really cute. The man is around forty with a touch of gray at his temples and pleasant blue eyes. I guess he's cute too, for a dad. He's holding a huge cake loaded with chocolate icing. It makes my mouth water.

Gramps and Mom appear from the kitchen.

"We're the Gilmores," the man says. "I think you have met my daughter, Jennifer, and this is my son, Colin. You can call me Gil. Everybody does. We have come to welcome you to our building."

"How nice," Mom says, taking the cake. "I'm Linda Blue. These are my children, David and Meggie, and this is my father, Sam Lane."

"Just call me Gramps. Everybody does," Gramps echoes Gil. "Won't you come in?"

"No, we didn't come to intrude on your evening meal," Gil says. "We'll visit another time. We just wanted to say welcome to Fashion City. We know you'll like it here. Everybody does."

"Why not come back and have dessert with us after dinner?" Mom suggests. "There is surely enough cake here for two families."

"Wouldn't that be nice?" Gil says, turning to Colin and Jennifer, who nod eagerly. As they leave us, I suspect that invitation was exactly what they were hoping for. With the Gilmores expected, we are excited at dinner. We can imagine we're really at home and everything is normal. Even the nuked meals aren't bad. The sight of the chocolate cake on the countertop makes me eat faster and clean my microwaveable plate. Afterward David and

I tidy up the kitchen quickly, then sit down in the living room to wait for the Gilmores. I manage to get to the door first when the bell rings.

"Tell us about yourselves," Gramps says to the Gilmores as we dig into the cake.

I'm not surprised that it tastes like an American cake, because I figure the ingredients are about the same—flour, sugar, eggs, butter. I like it. (Everybody does.)

Jennifer and Colin are sitting on either side of their father on one couch, while David and I sit with Mom on the other couch, with the coffee table conveniently arranged before us. Gramps sits in an armchair and balances his dessert dish on his knees.

"I'm in charge of programming at the television station," Gil says, "and the kids, of course, are still in school."

"But I'm turning sixteen this season, so I'll be joining the military," Colin says happily, as if he has announced he's going to the Super Bowl.

"Don't you want to go to college?" David blurts out.

There's no immediate response, just big-eyed stares, as if David has said something in Chromish.

"*I* certainly do," David adds, seeming a bit uncomfortable under their gaze.

"I will gladly give four years to serve the Fathers," Colin finally says. "And so should you, David."

"Four years is a long time," David says.

"At the age of sixteen in Fashion City every young man and woman joins the military," Colin explains. "They do it gladly. Of course, we don't have to fight for

· 111 ·

the first year. We're in training until the age of seventeen, when we go to the front lines."

"Front lines of what?" Gramps says.

"The war, of course," Colin says.

"What war?" Mom says.

"Whatever war we happen to be fighting at the time. People are always attacking the Land of the Fathers."

"What people?" Gramps persists. "What countries attack you?"

Colin shrugs.

"We don't know their names," Gil explains. "We don't need to know. They are people who hate us because they envy our freedoms and our way of life, and we have to defend our land. This is one way we can repay the Fathers for all they have done for us."

"And the girls go too?" I say, looking at Jennifer, who sits quietly eating her cake.

"Some of the girls are kept at home to tend the day care at the factories," Gil says. "When the time comes, we will apply for Jennifer to have that job so she won't have to fight. Your mom will no doubt do the same for you, Meggie. But there is much competition for those jobs."

He places an arm protectively across Jennifer's shoulders. She seems so delicate, it's impossible to picture her in military gear. I can't see Colin fighting either. He seems like the kind of kid who, on our Earth, would have kept his nose in a book or his eyes on a test tube.

"But I'm puzzled about something," Gil says. "You all ask so many questions that I thought you would already know the answers to." He speaks directly to Mom. "I'm sure, Linda, that things in Fashion City have changed somewhat since you lived here before the insurrection. You must have been very young when you left, and your kids were born in the Western Province." Then he turns to Gramps. "But it seems that you, sir, would remember the wars from having grown up here."

Oops. You can almost hear the wheels turning as each of us searches for an explanation. But as usual, it's Gramps who saves the day.

"I had a blow to the head that left me with amnesia," he tells the Gilmores, just as he told Joe, the telephone man. "I remember very little about Fashion City."

"And in a place like the Western Province"—David speaks up, trying too hard to be helpful—"we learned not to listen to the wild stories we heard from other people. There were some real wing nuts there. You know what I mean?"

"Wing nuts?" Gil says.

"Left wing, right wing, radicals?" David is out of his element. He wouldn't know a wing nut if it hit him in the head. Neither would Gil, is my bet.

There is silence in the room for a moment, as the Gilmores study our faces, and I wonder if we have blown our cover totally.

"I see," Gil says slowly, looking at Gramps. "Amnesia, huh? I have never known anybody with amnesia."

"Well, it's a bummer," Gramps says. "Makes you forget absolutely everything. Now, what were we discussing?"

I feel an attack of giggles coming on, but Mom reroutes my thoughts by jumping quickly back to the conversation.

"The young soldiers," she says, "they do come home at twenty, don't they?"

"If they live, yes, they are allowed to come home, as I did. But not everyone is so lucky," Gil says seriously.

Here I manage to put on a straight face.

"Sometimes they're killed," he continues. "That's the reality of war."

"Sure, they come home and go to work for the Fathers," Gramps says as he slaps his napkin irritably on the lamp table beside him. "Then they marry and have as many kids as possible, who will all wind up having the same life!"

The Gilmores are bewildered by Gramps's behavior, but only for a moment.

"I know what you're feeling," Gil says with a smile. Then he reaches into his shirt pocket, pulls out one of the blue Lotus pills wrapped in plastic, and hands it to Gramps.

"One Lotus for a difference you will notice," he says pleasantly. "Have one of mine."

"What the . . . ?" Gramps stares at the pill, and I think he starts to say a bad word, but he checks himself just in time. "No, thanks," he mumbles instead.

Gil shrugs and returns the pill to his pocket.

"Suppose Colin decides he doesn't want to go," Mom asks. "What then?"

"Of course Colin wants to go," Gil says sternly. "He has to go!"

Colin's face can't be read.

"The military police always get you," Jennifer says softly. "There's no way out."

The cake isn't as good as it was a few moments ago.

"That's too bad," Gramps says.

"I'm assuming things were different in the Western Province?" Gil says in a somewhat mocking tone. "Better, perhaps?"

Gramps sighs. "I suppose not."

"What's it really like over there?" Colin wants to know.

"Why did the Lincoln-King regime kill your husband?" Gil asks Mom.

"Did you really have to eat—you know—disgusting things?" comes from Jennifer.

There's a solemn pause before Mom says, "We prefer not to talk about it." After all, it had worked on Amanda Harp.

"Of course, of course," Gil says sympathetically. "It must have been awful."

There's silence again in the room, then Mom says with too much enthusiasm, "This is the most delicious cake I've ever tasted!"

While Gil is taking credit for baking the cake, and his kids are bragging about their dad's cooking skills, Gramps catches my eye and mumbles, "It's a nice change from eating rats." Then he winks at me, and once again, I have to stifle giggles. Fortunately, I don't think anybody else hears him.

At that moment I notice how Gil is smiling as he talks to Mom. Is he flirting with her? But, hey, why should I be surprised? I look at her in her Fashion City pants and an olive shirt that reads on the front YOU'LL LIKE IT HERE and on the back EVERYBODY DOES, and I can see that even in these cheesy threads, she looks pretty, in spite of being way over thirty.

· 17 ·

When everybody has finished with the cake, David and I gather the dirty dessert dishes, and Colin and Jennifer pretend to help by following us into the kitchen. Once there, of course, we linger for a while, apart from the adults.

"Do you guys play any kind of sports?" David asks as we settle around the table.

Again the blank faces.

"We're too old to play," Colin says. "Homemaking takes up much of our time."

Homemaking? But I won't go down that road. It sounds boring.

"And there's school, of course," he goes on.

"What level are you in?" I ask.

"I'm in seventh, the last level, and Jennifer's in sixth."

My eyes meet David's. Maybe we should have done

better on the test? It seems that David, at least, should be at Jennifer's level.

"How long do you stay in each level?" I ask.

"As long as it takes to finish," Colin responds. "It takes some people a short time and others a long time."

Could they *be* any more vague about time in this place?

"I gather we can't go to the park, except on specified days," David says. "But is it all right to go for a walk sometimes, you know, on the sidewalk?"

"Oh, certainly," Jennifer says. "A strong body serves the Fathers far better than a weak one. Walking is encouraged."

Her voice is monotonous, but her words are good to hear.

"So is biking, if you're lucky enough to have a bike," Jennifer continues. "As long as you don't neglect your work."

"And as long as you don't loiter or assemble in large groups," Colin adds.

"And why is that?"

"The insurrection, of course. Nobody wants a repeat of that."

"For sure," David mumbles.

Colin leans forward and whispers to David, "Can we trust you?"

"Trust me with what?" David says.

"With a secret."

"Oh, sure," David says, then looks at me and makes a zipping motion across his lips.

"Right," I say, and imitate my brother.

Colin whispers again, "I have a book." Then he smiles with pleasure at his guilty secret.

A book? *One* book?

"That's nice," David says. "What's it about?"

"It's about wolves. Did you know the Land of the Fathers used to be wild, with animals and vegetation? There were no people, except for a few primitive native tribes. Don't you find that fascinating?"

"Yeah, sure, fascinating," David says without much enthusiasm. "Which reminds me, we haven't seen any animals in Fashion City—like dogs or cats."

"There was a time when the people were allowed pets." Jennifer speaks up. "But as you must know, animals are filthy and carry disease."

"I think I've heard that," I say.

"Yes, they spread germs and attract fleas and ticks," Jennifer goes on. "That's why they were banned."

I almost roll my eyes but manage to control myself.

"I noticed that the stuffed animals at the mall are green and red and purple—all bright colors. Why is that?" I ask. "I mean, everything else in Fashion City is so . . . you know?"

"Right," Jennifer says. "As you can imagine, when the people of Fashion City had to give up their pets, they were very upset. To some of them, it was like losing a family member. We didn't have a pet because Mom was allergic, but I'll never forget that day when they brought around the trucks to carry away the animals."

"They took them all at once?" I say. "No way."

"Yeah, it was sad, especially for kids. Anyway, I think the Fathers felt bad," Jennifer explains. "They do love the people, you know."

"Sure they do," David mumbles, reminding me of Gramps.

"I mean, everything they do is for our own good," Jennifer says.

"Of course," I say.

"So, as a concession to those who were in mourning, they sent out all these stuffed animals in really bright colors. It cheered people up."

David and I don't know what to say. That's the most pitiful story ever. I don't even want to think about it.

"I still find animals very interesting," Colin says, "and I like to read about them, so please don't tell on me for the book. You see, this is one of the banned books from many years ago. We're not allowed to have them."

"Not allowed to have books?"

"Not like this one. The only approved books are instructional picture books for little kids, teaching them how to get along in our society."

"So how did you get this book about wolves?" I ask.

"A friend of mine purchased it for me. I didn't ask where he got it, probably from the black market."

"We certainly would never squeal on you," David says, "but do you go around telling just anybody?"

"Not just anybody," Colin replies. "There are informers among us, but after a while you learn to spot them. Besides, it's common knowledge that practically every family owns at least one banned book, some even more."

"Yeah," Jennifer says. "The police have almost given up trying to keep them out of our hands."

I am reminded of the sale of illegal drugs on the Earth we came from. Many people bought them in back alleys. I suppose that's something like the black market. But we're talking about *books* here, not drugs!

"Was that you guys we heard singing last night?" I ask, changing the subject.

"Yes!" Colin says. "We were singing 'Wild Hearts.' Did you like it?"

He looks at me with brilliant blue eyes, and my breath gets lost somewhere down there in my chest. It's the same feeling I had when Elvis was singing to me. Sure, I know Colin's nearly sixteen and I'm not even twelve yet, but a girl can dream.

"Yeah, I liked your song a lot," I tell him. "It was about wolves too, wasn't it?"

"Yeah. I wrote the lyrics and Dad wrote the music. We know all the approved songs—'You Are My Sunshine,' 'Tea for Two,' 'When I Fall in Love,' 'Some Enchanted Evening,' 'Love Is a Many-Splendored Thing'—but we get tired of them, so we write our own songs."

"Love Is a Many-Splendored Thing"? David and I used to gag a maggot over that one. We thought a song couldn't get any sappier. But, hey, if Colin sings it, maybe it's not *that* sappy.

"The Fathers encourage love songs because they want everybody to fall in love," Jennifer says.

I watch David's face go red. Yeah, he's a goner too.

"We practice together after lights-out," Colin says.

"Inside in cold weather, and on the balcony in warm weather."

"And is that allowed?" David asks.

"It's tolerated," Colin says. "A lot of people do it. After all, we're seven floors above the ground—six for you. I guess you've noticed that the apartments on the first floor don't have balconies. We're lucky."

"Most of the time we are quiet enough that we don't disturb anybody," Jennifer says.

"We'd love to hear you sing some more," David says. "Too bad we can't join you."

"Well, it so happens," Jennifer whispers excitedly, "Dad built a trapdoor in our balcony floor!"

"Jennifer!" Colin rebukes her. "Watch your mouth."

"Well, you told about your dumb old book!" Jennifer retorts hotly.

The two of them glare at each other for a moment, and it's obvious they don't always jell, just like David and me.

"Besides," Jennifer goes on, "Meggie and David are okay. I can tell."

"Actually," Colin says, turning back to me and David, "what we do in our own homes is private. The Fathers would never allow a search of our apartment without suspicion of serious crimes."

"Anyway," Jennifer goes on, "we used to slip down through the trapdoor in the dark after lights-out, to visit the family who lived here before you."

"What happened to them?"

"They had more children, and were given nicer

quarters in Sector D. Those apartments are much roomier. The Fathers are pleased with large families."

"And did you sing with that family?"

"No, they didn't care much for singing, but we still had fun together."

"Well, we care a lot for singing," David says. "I'll ask Mom if you can come down to our balcony after lights-out."

"Do you know some songs you could teach us?" Colin asks.

"Hundreds!" David says. "Gramps says that American music is one of the wonders of the universe."

David bites his lip. Colin and Jennifer are obviously puzzled.

"What kind of music is that?" Colin asks.

David doesn't know what to say, so I speak up. "That's Gramps for you. He has his own name for everything. Sometimes it's like listening to a foreign language."

"What's a foreign language?" Colin asks.

Again David and I glance at each other. It's clear we're going to have to think before saying anything, and measure and weigh every word.

"Never mind," David says, and changes the subject again. "Where's your mom?"

Now it's Colin and Jennifer who glance at each other.

"She . . . she's not with us anymore," Colin says.

At this moment we hear Tom down the hall. "Eight-thirty lockdown!"

As we join the adults in the living room, Gil is already on his feet.

"It's been a pleasure," he says. "Curfew, kids. Let's go."

In the next moment the Gilmores are gone, and the four of us are left standing there staring at each other with more questions than we'll ever have answers for.

"Are they robots or what?" Gramps says.

"Programmed to the nth," Mom says, then adds, "We'll be leaving here ASAP."

"Yeah," Gramps agrees. "I think we can find a more suitable place to live in this great big universe."

Tom comes ringing at our door, and after his check, *The Family Hour* screeches in our ears like fingernails on a chalkboard, but tonight I don't let it bother me because all I can see is Colin's face, and all I can hear is his voice.

Robot or not, he's totally hot.

· 18 ·

The next day I set aside thoughts of the Carriage computer and I rush through my schoolwork so that David and I can go for a walk with Colin and Jennifer. At the end of the period, we meet in the lobby of Building 9 and head toward the business area of town. It's a really pretty day, and lots of people are out walking. They speak to us as we pass them on the street, and I can almost imagine that we're back in our friendly North Carolina town. We stop for a soft drink, which Colin pays for, at a sidewalk café. He gives me a breathtaking smile as he hands my drink to me. I think he *likes* likes me.

A few minutes later we come to a long black granite wall, on which names are chiseled in fine white print.

"It's the Wall of the Fallen," Colin explains in a solemn voice as he places one hand against the granite.

"It shows the names of those brave ones from Fashion City who have died for the Fathers."

"In the wars, you mean?" I ask.

Colin nods. He stands very still, and I wonder if he's imagining *Colin Gilmore* added to this long list. Even though I was warm a moment ago, now I find myself shivering.

I glance through the list, and find common, ordinary names of all nationalities. I wonder if there's a Germany and an England and an Australia on this Earth. What about China? India? Did natives of other countries emigrate to the Land of the Fathers as they did to America on our Earth? Were black people brought here from Africa as slaves? Are we even on a continent that's shaped like North America?

David interrupts my thoughts suddenly by crying out, "George Herman Ruth!"

On our Earth we knew him as Babe Ruth. He's one of David's heroes. According to the wall, he died at the age of eighteen fighting for the Fathers. In this place he never had a chance, never set a home run record, probably never even learned to play baseball.

"Walter Elias Disney!" David gasps. "Age nineteen!"

No Walt Disney? No Mickey Mouse. No Disneyland.

"Laura Elizabeth Ingalls!" It's my turn to gasp. "Age seventeen!"

On this planet she never married Almanzo Wilder, and the Little House books were never written.

Colin and Jennifer are obviously mystified.

"You know these people?" Colin asks.

David and I can't speak. I think both of us are momentarily in shock, or mourning. We leave the Wall of the Fallen quickly. I never want to see it again. I don't want to know the names of any more people who never had a chance to fulfill their dreams and live out their lives the way they wanted to.

After lights-out, my family and the Gilmores meet on our balcony as planned. David has the nerve to sit right down beside Jennifer on a blanket with her dad and Colin, while I sit on another blanket with Mom and Gramps. Still, we're all pretty close together in this small space. In fact, I could reach right out and touch Colin—that is, if I wanted to make a big fool of myself.

We can hear people chatting on the other balconies near us, but we can't tell who it is or what they're saying. I'm glad we're six floors up from the ground.

As soon as Gil begins playing his guitar and singing solo on the first verse of "Wild Hearts," I can sense the Gilmores' tensions melting away. The music lifts them right out of themselves, out of this screwy world and into a happier place, at least in their minds. Now they seem like regular people.

Gramps and Mom begin to hum along with them, while David and I clap our hands in time. It's not a fast, happy song, but it does have a steady beat. Of course, they're amateurs, but I imagine that on our Earth this family could make a career with their music, maybe even become famous.

When the song ends, Mom, Gramps, David, and I applaud enthusiastically. The Gilmores are beaming with pride. The next thing I know we are talking and joking around like we've been friends for years. Although we're in the dark, I can hear Colin's laughter and imagine his face. Tonight he's not thinking of war.

"Okay, Blues," he says. "We want to learn new songs. What can you teach us?"

" 'The Lion Sleeps Tonight,'" I say. "It's the best one."

"Let's hear it," Gil says, and strums his guitar.

"That's a hard one, Meggie," Mom says. "Remember how many wacky sounds are mixed into it?"

"It's okay," Jennifer tells us. "Dad's good. He can pick out the chords and play anything you can sing."

So, between us, David and I are able to recall all the lyrics to "The Lion Sleeps Tonight," but we find out that Mom is right. This is a hard one. Still, we try. We get Gramps to sing the lead while David and I do some of the background parts, and hand out others to Mom and the Gilmores. Pretty soon we are all laughing so hard, we can't even hit the right notes, and Gil has to tell us to hold it down so the night watchman won't order us to bed.

"They don't ever say anything to us for being out here," he explains, "but that doesn't mean they won't."

"Okay," Mom says in an exaggerated whisper. "Let's do a nice, quiet one."

" 'Bridge over Troubled Water,'" Gramps says. "It's my favorite. I like to call it the secular Twenty-third Psalm."

"What does that mean?" Gil asks.

But Gramps jumps right into the song so that he doesn't have to answer Gil. Mom, David, and I help him with the words, but Gramps has a pretty strong voice, and manages to carry the melody, while Gil picks up the chords.

When the song is over, Gil says, "Those are the most moving lyrics I've ever heard."

"Okay," David says brightly, trying to raise the mood. "And now for something a little different. Help me, Meggie."

He wants to do Justin Bieber's "Baby." So together we try to sing, but we have a hard time remembering all the words, and even the tune in some places. To make matters worse, David's voice cracks twice and I can feel how mortified he is. Still, this seems to be the turning point for Jennifer and David. It's obvious he has impressed her.

"That was sooo marvelous, Daavid." She stretches his name out like it has three syllables, and her voice is very girly-girly. I imagine David's heart is thundering like a timpani. "And you too, Meggie," she goes on. "Please teach me that song."

But Colin says nothing.

I'm guessing it must be midnight when we reluctantly part, and only then because Mom reminds us that she and Gramps have been called to report to work at eight tomorrow morning. Gil, of course, has to go to his job at the TV station as well. So the Gilmores dutifully climb up through their trapdoor, and we promise to meet again tomorrow evening to sing in the darkness.

"I guess they're not robots after all," Gramps says as we grope our way down the hallway to our bedrooms.

"Not tonight," Mom agrees. "They were fun, and a breath of fresh air in this stuffy place."

The next day, after my lessons are done, I take the Carriage computer out of the backpack in the closet, prop it up in the center of my bed, and do a search on Chroma. I find more than I can read at one sitting, so I begin with the Blue race. I have just settled in to read when I hear Colin and Jennifer in the living room. I put the computer away quickly and join them. A few days ago I was bored, with nothing to do, and now I wonder if there will be enough hours in the day.

Colin has brought the book he's so proud of, stashed under his shirt. It is, as he said, about wolves and the Land of the Fathers before the age of industrialization. There are no specifics in it, no names of places or people that we can relate to, and when we check to see when or where it was published, we find there's no information.

Mom and Gramps come home shortly after five o'clock. They say the work at the factory isn't hard, but it's repetitive and boring.

"And you're not allowed to call us there," Mom says. "I'm sorry." She closes her eyes briefly and bites her lip, then goes on, "So if you ever need help, you'll have to call Tom. That's part of his job."

"When do you get a day off?" I ask.

They look at each other and say nothing.

"You have to work every single day?" David says. "How can they do that to you?"

"We'll be allowed days off when it's necessary to visit the health clinic, also to go to the park with you when it's our turn," Gramps says.

"And that's all?" David sputters.

"As we told you," Mom says, "the work's not difficult."

But she can't disguise that gloomy look on her face. "We can stick with it for a little while," Mom goes on, "until we figure out our next move."

"Not to worry, Meggie B.," Gramps tells me. "Let's consider Fashion City like one of those rest areas where we used to stop on the interstate. We are resting before we get back into our vehicle and move on."

"I think they are afraid we might wind up in a worse place than this," David later confides to me. "They know only the basics of programming the Carriage navigator."

"But Mom was a really smart professor!" I protest. "Wasn't she trained to navigate the Carriage?"

"You probably don't remember, since you were only three," David says, "but it was Gramps who took the training before we left Chroma. Mom was spending all her time with Dad in his last days."

That bit of information makes me nervous, because I know Mom is the technology geek in our family, while Gramps is the artiste.

The next day, I search the computer and find a tutorial for the Carriage. Could I? Of course I could. Why not? Yes! I'm going to learn all by myself to navigate this space thingy, and you know what? I can do it, because *I* understand the language.

· 19 ·

David Speaks

L iving in the Land of the Fathers, we settled into rou-
tine. We don't feel the same bliss that Ulysses's men
felt in their lotus stupor, but we are temporarily recon-
ciled to the idea of living in this mundane world.

Mom and Gramps go to work early each day, while
Meggie and I take care of the apartment and do the food
shopping. We've learned that in Fashion City boys and
girls our age are expected to develop homemaking skills
in preparation for having a family someday. In the after-
noons we obediently do our monotonous schoolwork. For
some reason Meggie's class lasts longer than mine. Then
we go for a walk with Colin and Jennifer, or if the
weather is bad, we meet inside. Sometimes we go to their
place, which is exactly like ours, but usually, just out of
habit, we gather at our place.

Gil has decided that our night group will always meet

on our balcony, because he says it's inconsiderate to expect Mom and Gramps to climb up through the trapdoor. Sure, it's nice of him, but if he'd ever seen Mom and Gramps doing chin-ups or playing sports with me and Meggie, he'd know Mom is no buttercup and Gramps isn't feeble. Still, it's okay with us, so we let Gil be the gentleman and have his way.

Jennifer is a shining star in this otherwise dreary world. In fact, I'm torn between wanting to be with her and wanting to leave this place forever. Which do I want more? I can't say. I've been so wrapped up in her spell, it's taken me a while to notice Meggie's crush on Colin. As her big brother, I feel obligated to discourage her—for her own good, of course.

"You know, he's not interested in a girl your age," I tell her one day.

"I'm little, but I'm old," she says to me.

"That line was so much funnier when Dill said it in *To Kill a Mockingbird*," I tell her, just to make her aware that I know those words are not original with her.

"You know what I mean," she says. "Our minds are equal."

I have to laugh at that. "Why, you haven't even achieved blue yet," I remind her—once again.

"Blue means nothing to him," she says. "Furthermore, you dork, it means nothing to me either. In this world, it'll only get you in trouble."

I chuckle because I know she doesn't really feel that way. I'm not blind to her habit of checking the mirror two or three times a day. She's dying to see blue.

But Meggie's crush on Colin isn't nearly as hysterical as Gil's crush on Mom. He is sooo obvious, it's embarrassing. He picks up small gifts for her—chocolates, flowers, a fruit basket. Yuck. Yuck. Yuck. And both of them pushing forty.

Occasionally we come across Bonnie, the woman next door who is afflicted with gross vacillation, and we see Tom each evening at lockdown, or when he's collecting schoolwork. Sometimes he brings our work back to us for corrections, but only when we've been careless. We'd have to be in a coma to have real problems with these classes.

We've met only a few of the other tenants in our building. Colin and Jennifer told us there aren't many young people living here, and no small children at all.

"As soon as a new baby is born, they move," Jennifer explains. "Everybody but us seems to be moving up."

Meggie doesn't care much for food shopping, and I certainly don't like dusting and vacuuming, so we trade off, and that's how I wind up doing most of the grocery shopping by myself.

Often Tammy pushes a few of the blue boxes into my hands. "Take some of these today," she says with a goofy Lotus smile. "One Lotus for a difference you'll notice."

I accept them because I feel like I can't refuse. Mom tells me not to pick up the stuff on my own, but if it's offered, I should accept. We've collected so many boxes, we have nowhere to store them, and when you open a kitchen cabinet, they come tumbling down on you.

One evening Meggie mentions that Gil eats Lotus like it's candy.

"Maybe it's because he's in 'luv,'" I say, and I'm surprised to see Mom blushing a little. "I'm amazed he hasn't proposed to you yet," I tease her. "You know the Fathers want everybody in pairs."

"He's very nice," Mom says, "and he has a lovely singing voice. But I wouldn't have a husband who allows himself to be manipulated with drugs and mind control."

"He has no choice," Gramps says. "He doesn't have the option to leave, as we have."

The next day Colin and Jennifer come in wearing shorts.

"Hey, Meggie B.," Colin says with a smile, and I can see her eyes glaze over. He has used her pet name, and I know she must be daydreaming that he feels the same way she does, but I know he's just being nice to a kid.

"It's a hot day, David," Jennifer interrupts my thoughts. "Are you going to be comfortable in jeans?"

"Yeah, it's a real scorcher," Colin agrees. "Better dress cool."

"We didn't see any shorts for sale at the mall," I say.

"They were there," Jennifer explains. "But maybe you missed them because they don't have much of a selection."

Duh! Like they have a good selection of anything. But I keep that thought to myself.

"I'll ask Mom to buy some," Meggie says, "but today, jeans it is."

"Then why don't we just stay indoors?" Colin suggests.

"I agree," I say. "No point in being miserable."

"Good idea," says Jennifer. "Do you guys have a radio?"

We don't, so Jennifer goes upstairs to bring theirs down, while the rest of us settle around the kitchen table.

"You should get a radio," Colin tells us. "It pleases the Fathers."

"What kind of programs do you listen to?" I ask.

"They play nothing but music all day long," Colin says. "It's nice."

"Great!" I say, and I mean it, but my joy is short-lived. When Jennifer plugs in the radio, elevator music pours out of it. It's worse than church music, but I suppose it's better than no music at all—barely. With the music as a backdrop, we settle into a nice, normal conversation— uh, as normal as conversations go in Fashion City.

After a while Colin says, "Our dad is going to marry your mother. Of course, I'll soon be gone to war, but the rest of you will get larger quarters, and it'll be good for everybody."

I'm surprised, and slightly ticked off to hear him say this. As far as I know, Gil hasn't asked Mom, and Colin is surely taking a lot for granted.

"I don't think Mom will ever marry again," I tell him.

Jennifer is astonished. "Not marry? The Fathers won't be pleased."

"Right," Colin agrees. "Your mom is young enough to have more kids."

"I don't think Mom wants more kids!" I say hotly. "The Fathers just want more workers and soldiers. And by the way, do the Fathers send their own children to war?"

"The children of the Fathers at war!" Jennifer exclaims, as if I'm being irrational. "They are much too valuable as our future leaders. Look at all the sacrifices the Fathers have made for us already."

"That's absurd!" I say. "Why don't we ever see these Fathers? Where do they live? Certainly not in the sectors. No, they are out of sight so that we can't see their elaborate lifestyle. And it's for sure that, wherever they are, their rivers are not polluted with factory waste, and the air they breathe is not thick enough to stick to the lungs."

Jennifer is so distraught at my words, she takes a Lotus pill from her shorts pocket, unwraps it with unsteady fingers, and chews it.

"The Fathers take care of the people," she says. "Praise the Fathers."

I've upset her, and now I feel like a jerk. So I try to backtrack. "Just sayin' . . . but look, I didn't mean anything."

Colin stands up, unplugs the radio, and tucks it under one arm. "Jennifer, we should go."

Jennifer nods and stands up as well.

At the door, Colin turns and says to me in a low, controlled voice, "Your newness in our city is wearing off, and you must learn quickly that you can't say things like that. It's not tolerated."

"You can be sent away for disloyal statements," Jennifer adds.

"Sent away where?"

"To wherever they sent Mom," Jennifer answers as tears well up in her eyes.

· 20 ·

Back to Meggie

I dig further into the Carriage tutorial and learn that the navigation is done by figuring a set of coordinates. It's a string of numbers that's like a code that you punch into the control panel. The first number is for the place you're located, and the numbers after that are for something else, followed by a number for the planet of your destination, then the latitude and longitude numbers for the location on that planet, then a more specific number, then something . . . something that I haven't quite figured out yet.

If you have no specific destination, and you want the computer to find a place for you, you enter your preferences. That's what Gramps did when he brought us here, and obviously it's not the best method. I imagine that's why Mom and Gramps are now nervous about moving forward. They want to find just the right place next time, and considering all the possible worlds out there, it's not easy.

David knocks on my door. "Jennifer and Colin are here."

As I store the computer, I realize I didn't finish my schoolwork. Well, so what? I haven't messed up since I've been here. I place the half-finished work in the door pocket for Tom.

Both Colin and Jennifer are in a good mood as we set off toward the city. Maybe they each had a Lotus for a difference we'd notice. They seem not to remember David's dissing of the Fathers yesterday. Pretending all's well is a habit of most people here.

Today there's a mild breeze, like rain may be in the air, and we agree to a shorter walk than usual. We're on our way back home when the thunder starts.

Colin points in the direction of some apartment buildings we haven't seen before. "Let's take a shortcut through these parking lots over here!" he suggests.

"The dark people live here," Jennifer explains.

"So the African . . . I mean, the black people live apart from whites?" I ask.

"Yes, of course," Colin says. "The Fathers don't allow the races to mix."

I know America didn't integrate overnight. It was tough, and there were "years and years of fears and tears," as my African American teacher used to say, but they made a lot of progress. It seems the people in this place haven't even started to work on the race problem. Could it be because they have no leadership since Lincoln and King left to go to the Western Province?

As rain begins to hit the pavement in large crystal drops, several young black girls hurry around a corner and head into one of the buildings. That's when I see her.

"Kitty!" The words burst out of me, and I run to her. "Kitty! It *is* you!"

I become aware of two things at once—David clutching my arm and pulling me away, and Kitty looking at me with puzzled brown eyes. "Who are you?"

"Sorry," David mumbles to her. "My sister mistook you for somebody else."

"But my name *is* Kitty!" she calls after us. "How did you know?"

David holds my arm tightly and leads me to where Colin and Jennifer are waiting.

"Well, anyhow," Kitty calls again. "I like your shoes!"

My shoes? I realize then for the first time since coming to this planet that my sneakers are different from everybody else's, and nobody but Kitty has noticed. Of course the shoes are white—now a dirty white—like almost all the others, but they have purple laces with a gold star dangling from each lace. On our Earth, Kitty picked them out for me one day when we were in town together.

As David pulls me along, I look back once more to see Kitty, and she is staring after me curiously. I watch until her familiar face is blurred by the gray slant of the rain.

"What was that all about?" Jennifer asks as we slog along toward home.

But I pretend not to hear her.

Naturally, when I tell Mom about seeing Kitty, she's sympathetic but firm. She orders me to stay away from the black area.

"I don't think you understand that we have no rights here, Meggie," she explains. "No matter how much we object to their ways, we have to follow the rules."

I know Mom is right, but I *have* to see Kitty. I'll be careful. I will *not* get caught.

The next day, after our walk, I slip out of the apartment and return to the black district. For a long time I stand some distance away from Kitty's building and watch. I give up and start toward home, but then suddenly there she is, running on the sidewalk, wearing her favorite purple shirt. She has a bag slung across her shoulder. Her face is wet with sweat, and her breath comes in ragged gasps.

"Kitty!" I cry.

"I need a place to hide!" she pants, her eyes darting frantically. "Please help me!"

Without a thought of danger, I pull Kitty down a narrow alley. A doorway stands open in the wall. I push her through it, and we find ourselves in a murky storage room. It's semidark and smells of rotting vegetables. Quietly I close the door behind us, and we hug the cool plaster wall.

"They're after me," Kitty whispers, and wipes her face on the purple shirt.

"Who?"

"The police. One more offense and I'll be sent away."

"What have you done?" I ask.

"You name it! I've been to rehab so many times, it's a wonder I don't have a serious case of gross vacillation. But you know what? They can't warp my mind! Never! It's the only thing I have that's really mine."

Then she laughs that familiar laugh, and it does my heart good to hear it.

"They call me incurable!" she adds.

"You always were!" I agree.

Her smile is replaced by a look of bewilderment. " 'Always'? What does that mean?"

"Oh, nothing." For a moment there I forgot this was not my own good friend Kitty but a duplicate of her on a parallel Earth. "I just meant that I can tell by that shirt that you're one of a kind."

"Don'tcha just love it?" Kitty says.

"Yes, I love it."

"I made it myself! I was walking past the garbage outside the factory and saw the cloth. Can you imagine throwing away something as cool as this?"

"How do you get away with wearing it?"

"I can run like the wind."

We both tense as footsteps pass outside the door, then fade away.

"What's your name?" Kitty whispers.

"Meggie Blue. I'm new here."

"New?" she says. "Meggie Blue? How do you do? Meggie Blue's new."

We both laugh, and it's on the tip of my tongue to say "And do you do voodoo?" but I resist.

"I haven't met a new person in a long time," she goes on. "How did you know my name yesterday?"

I hedge. "Oh, I just guessed. You look like a Kitty."

She laughs. "If you say so. Now guess what I'm going to be when I grow up."

It's a strange comment coming from a Fashion City girl.

"I don't know," I say. "A clothing store clerk, maybe?"

She laughs again. "At least you didn't say a factory worker! I'm going to be a fashion designer. Do you think that's crazy?"

"No."

"But only the Fathers actually design the clothes. Whoever heard of a factory worker's daughter doing such a thing?"

"All good things start with a dream," I say.

"That's so true!" Kitty says excitedly. "But they try to make us believe that the daydreamer is discontented."

I can almost hear *The Family Hour* repeating, "Conformity is contentment. The daydreamer is discontented." But I won't let these words sway me, because I don't believe them. Gramps has told me that's how brainwashing happens. They put their words into your head, and those words automatically spring to mind when the right button is pushed. But Gramps has also told me that some people have such a strong sense of self, they can't be brainwashed. Now it seems to me that Kitty is such a person.

"The factories are divided into public parts and secret

parts," Kitty says. "And when my mom was with me, she was so good, they let her work in the secret part."

"Your mom isn't with you anymore?"

"No, she and my dad were sent away for book hoarding," Kitty says sadly. "They had so many books that even Mom's talent couldn't save them when they were caught. Now I live with my grandpa."

Book lovers in two separate worlds. The other Kitty's parents were librarians.

"Anyhow, Mom's factory job was hand-stitching dresses for the families of the Fathers. She told me that nobody could imagine how beautiful and colorful the dresses were. But *I* can imagine them. I see them in my head, and I try to draw them. And I bought these magazines today. I saved rations and tokens forever to pay for them!"

She opens her bag and shows me four copies of a glossy high-fashion magazine.

"Wow!" I say. "Will you get into trouble for having these?"

"You better believe it!" she says. "That's why the police were after me. They arrested the dealer, but they couldn't catch me!"

We hear voices in another room, and move cautiously toward the door we entered by.

"I think we're in the storage room of a grocery store," Kitty whispers again. "We better get out before we're busted."

I ease the door open and peep into the street.

"No police," I say to Kitty. "But you know what? They can spot that shirt a mile off. How about turning it inside out? The other side is probably not as brilliant, is it?"

"No, it's not," Kitty says. "Good thinking!"

She sets her bag down, slips the shirt off quickly, turns it inside out, and slips it back on. Then we venture onto the street again.

"Well, strange new white girl," she says as we walk toward her building. "You better be on your way, hadn't you?"

"Why?"

"Because if they see you with me, you'll be in double trouble."

"How so?" I ask.

"You know, the white face, black face thing!"

"Oh, I see."

"And then there's the fact that I'm a hunted criminal."

I laugh. "You're no criminal!"

We part ways, and when I turn to wave at Kitty, she has turned also to wave at me.

I can't resist calling to her, "Hey, Kitty! Do you know a guy named Corey Marshall?"

Her mouth falls open and she stops walking. "Girl! How'd you know 'bout him?"

I laugh. "See you around, Kitty!"

· 21 ·

When I arrive home, Mom and Gramps are both pacing
the floor.

"Where have you been?" Mom says sharply. "I was sick
with worry!"

"I'm not a baby!" I say. "I know my way around."

"But this place, Meggie, this place . . ." She can't finish that thought. "I don't think you understand what they
can do to you."

"Meggie, child," Gramps says kindly, "did you go see
Kitty?"

I nod.

"Please promise me, Meggie, that you won't do it
again."

"I promise," I mumble, but Mom and Gramps give
each other a helpless look. We all know it's a promise I
can't keep.

"Well, there's another matter to discuss," Mom says wearily as she rubs her temples. "When I arrived home from work today, Tom handed me a note from the education center."

"And what did it say?" As if I don't know.

"You haven't been doing all of your schoolwork."

"Just one day." I try not to sound whiny, but I don't think I'm successful. "Only one time I didn't finish, and that was yesterday."

"Once is too many times," Mom goes on. "They're giving you a warning."

"What does that mean?"

"If it happens again, they're going to send over a tutor, and according to Tom, you do *not* want a tutor."

She puts so much emphasis on the word *not* that I totally believe her.

"Apparently the tutors are mean and they're tough," Mom goes on, "and they'll stay with you for hours if they have to. You don't want to deal with that, Meggie."

"It won't happen again," I say quickly.

At dinner David asks Mom if we can buy a radio. "They play music all day," he says. "Maybe not our kind of music, but it's better than nothing."

"I beg to differ," Gramps says. "No music at all is better."

"What does that mean?"

"One of the men at work is a kind of rebel, if you can believe it," Gramps says. "In fact, I think he's bound to be arrested soon, and I'm almost afraid to be seen talking to him—you know, the guilt by association thing. Anyhow, he told me that the radio music is packed full of subliminal messages."

"What's a subliminal message?" I ask.

"It's a message that's taped along with the music, but at a different speed. When the tape is played, the conscious mind hears only the music, while the subconscious picks up the underlying message."

"No kidding!" David says, and I'm surprised that Gramps has actually told my brother something he doesn't already know.

"No kidding," Gramps said. "It's just another way to brainwash the unfortunate people of Fashion City."

"So that's why the Fathers want everybody to have a radio," I say.

"Probably so," Mom says, "and I guess we should buy one just to look good. We don't have to play it."

When *The Family Hour* comes on, Mom and Gramps plug toilet paper into their ears to drown out the noise— not that it does much good—and set the Carriage computer up at the kitchen table.

"When do I get to learn how to drive the family car?" David calls above the racket.

"As soon as Gramps and I are confident enough in our own knowledge," Mom calls back. "We want to make sure you learn properly."

I hope nobody looks at me, because I feel guilt written all over my face.

"That's cool," David says. "Driver's ed at thirteen."

On *The Family Hour*, Sherry Cross is saying, "We have two arrests to report tonight. Forty-four-year-old Jorge

Mendez of Sector F was arrested for black-market dealing in an alley near the black sectors. And eleven-year-old Kathryn Singer of Sector J was turned in by her grandfather for buying merchandise from the same dealer. It's the fifth arrest for this young person, and regretfully her luck has run out. She will be sent away for an indefinite period."

Kitty's tear-streaked face flashes on the screen, and Mom cries, "Oh, no! Kitty!"

"That scoundrel Henry Singer!" Gramps says angrily. "He turned in his own granddaughter?"

We don't sing with the Gilmores that night. Mom begs off with a headache. Then she and Gramps study the Carriage tutorial far into the night, while I lie awake with Kitty's face shimmering before me like a scene from a sad movie playing over and over.

· 22 ·

Of course we can't tell the Gilmores about Kitty. When we're on the balcony with them the next evening, I try not to think of her, and it's difficult, but I'm cheered by the singing, for this is the evening we teach our friends to sing "Over the Rainbow." All three of them simply fall in love with this song, probably because it implies that a heavenly place exists beyond Fashion City.

"I know it will stay in my head for days and days," Jennifer says dreamily.

I think of *The Wizard of Oz*, in which Judy Garland sang the song. Kitty and I watched it together one stormy Saturday. Wouldn't the Fashion City Kitty and the Gilmores absolutely love it? But my new friends will never know Dorothy and the marvelous cowardly lion, or the tin man and the scarecrow.

"It's a lovely night, isn't it?" Gil says softly to Mom as he moves closer to her.

It's comical the way Mom jumps and starts talking in a loud, nervous voice.

"Officer Brent told us something peculiar on that first day," she says. "He said there's no poverty, no disease, and no violent crime in Fashion City. How can that be?"

"The Fathers would never allow us to live in poverty," Gil says. "And the curfew has much to do with the lack of violence."

"What about disease?" Mom goes on hurriedly. "Surely the Fathers have not found a way to completely wipe it all out?"

"No, but we have regular checkups, and we get vaccinations, and medication for whatever ails us. We're also advised about exercise and diet. The Fathers take care of the people."

"But we haven't seen a single handicapped person. Are there none?" Mom goes on. "And what of serious diseases such as cancer, heart disease, stroke, Parkinson's—you know, really debilitating illnesses?"

"People who are too dysfunctional to contribute to our society are sent away to the hospital of the Fathers, where they are cured."

"Completely cured?"

"Yes."

"Then do they come back to their families?"

"Oh, no, they never come back."

Gramps guffaws loudly. "Imagine that!" he says. "They never come back!"

"Why not?" Mom asks. "If they're cured, why can't they live normally?"

Gil obviously doesn't know how to answer Mom's question, and he seems irritated with Gramps, so he solves both problems by popping a Lotus.

"Praise the Fathers!" he says.

"For they are good," Colin and Jennifer add automatically.

"And why must they be sent away to the hospital of the Fathers?" Mom persists. "Are there no hospitals here in Fashion City?"

"No, that would not be practical," Gil says. "Hospitals are very expensive to run."

"You mean too expensive for unimportant people like us?" Gramps asks.

"Quite right," Gil says, totally missing the ridiculousness of Gramps's words. "Consider how much it would cost to have hospitals and doctors in all the cities."

Though we have picked up bits and pieces of information about other cities, this is the first time the Gilmores have mentioned them. Gramps jumps onto that topic.

"What other cities are there?"

"I've heard there is a Food City, Auto City, Technology City, Furniture City, and . . . I don't know all of them. And oh, yeah, there's Warfare City. It's the most important one."

"Indeed!" Gramps exclaims.

"Did all the cities have rebels involved in the insurrection?" Mom asks.

"Yes. All of them," Gil says. "It was a well-coordinated revolt."

"Are the other cities anything like Fashion City?" Gramps asks.

I wonder if Mom and Gramps are asking too many questions. Surely these facts are common knowledge in the Western Province, where we supposedly came from.

But Gil answers. "Exactly like it."

"That's too bad," Gramps mutters.

That's when Gil bristles. "Why don't you ever talk about the Western Province?"

"Yeah," Colin joins in. "You've said next to nothing about your life there."

"You question so many things in our society," Gil says, "it makes me wonder if you were better off there."

"Why did you come here?" Jennifer adds.

"Fair questions, but I'm sorry we can't answer them right now," Mom says.

"Why not?" Gil persists.

"In time," Gramps finally says without sarcasm, "perhaps we will be able to tell you of our lives there. But not now."

"So it was not better than here?" Gil keeps pushing.

Nobody answers him.

"Never mind," Gil says abruptly. "For whatever reason, it appears you're not entirely candid with us."

"I could say the same about you, Gil, in regard to your wife," Mom says. "I find it strange that you never mention her, or tell us what happened to her."

It's Gil's turn to clam up.

"The children said she was sent away," Gramps says. "What did she do?"

"It's okay," Mom says softly. "I think we all have a right to our secrets."

Only a few minutes later, the Gilmores call it a night and leave us.

The next evening, David, peeved that he didn't get to spend more time with Jennifer the night before, is determined not to let the same arguments come up again. In no time he has us in stitches with his impersonation of the crabby announcer on The Family Hour, whose name, we have learned, is Andrew Andrews.

"If it's yellow, let it mellow!" David says grumpily in his Andrew Andrews voice. "But if it's brown, flush it down!"

When we have stopped laughing, the Gilmores teach "Wild Hearts" to us. Then Gil sings "Bridge over Troubled Water" in his rich tenor voice. I have the feeling he's singing it to impress Mom, and I'm guessing she really likes it.

I don't know how to feel about Mom and Gil. It's like two parts of me are struggling with each other. First there's the part of me that doesn't want to share Mom with anybody else, and then there's the part that remembers her crying for Dad on the porch in North Carolina when she thought I was asleep. If Mom learned to love Gil back, could he heal her sadness? And would she forget Dad? I don't *want* her to forget Dad.

"The moon is almost full," Gil says to her when he has

finished singing and has laid his guitar aside, "but there are so many clouds we don't get all of its lovely light."

By that pale moonlight we can see him take one of Mom's hands in his. "I have a serious question to ask you in private," he says to her in a low voice. "Perhaps you will go inside with me for a moment?"

"No, no, I . . ." Mom obviously has no good excuse, so she just says "No" again, then removes her hand from his.

"Very well, then I'll ask you here," Gil declares. "I would like to marry you."

Total silence falls over our group. I feel sorry for Mom, but even sorrier for Gil. He'll be rejected in front of his kids. But Mom says nothing right away.

"Our children get along well," he continues, "and I'm sure we can move to larger quarters in a nicer sector. Gramps, of course, is welcome to live with us. It would be pleasant for all of us."

"No, I can't do that," Mom says, then adds kindly, "but I do appreciate your offer."

It's obvious that Gil did not expect a refusal. He seems stunned.

"But why not?" he wants to know. "Give me one good reason!"

"I don't *want* to marry again," Mom states simply.

"What's wrong with you!" he blurts out.

"Nothing's wrong with me," Mom responds. "Am I not free to make that choice?"

"For a short period of time, yes," Gil admits. "But you're young and healthy. The Fathers won't allow you to stay single. You should jump at this chance, as you don't know what kind of man you'll be forced to accept later on."

"No offense to you, Gil," Mom says calmly, "but do you know how absurd that sounds?"

"Absurd?" Gil says. "I don't understand you. It seemed we were moving in that direction. I thought we were getting along so well—I mean, not counting last night."

"We do get along, and I enjoy your company," Mom says. "We all enjoy being with you and your family. It makes the days bearable. And I value your friendship."

"But you won't marry me?" he says sadly.

"That's right. We want to remain friends with you and your family, but marriage is out of the question. Please accept my decision."

"Of course," Gil says softly. "I don't want to lose your friendship."

And it seems the matter is settled.

· 23 ·

David Speaks

The day after Gil's embarrassing proposal to Mom, a policeman stops Meggie while we're out walking.

"Grossly unique," he says, and points to her shoes.

Uh-oh. He has spotted the purple laces with gold stars.

"Oh," Meggie says, seeming uncertain what to say or do. "Well, I won't wear them again."

The policeman is persistent. He holds out a hand. "Give them to me."

"You want me to take them out now?" Meggie says.

"Yes."

Meggie glances at Colin, but he looks away. She turns to me.

"How's she going to keep her shoes on her feet without laces?" I ask.

"That's her problem," the cop replies.

There's nothing to do but obey. Meggie sits down on the curb, removes the laces from her shoes, and hands them to the cop. He stuffs them into his pocket and walks away without another word.

"He'll probably keep them for his own kid," Meggie blurts out.

"Shut up!" Colin says rudely, and glances at the retreating back of the policeman. "If he hears, you'll *really* be in trouble."

Now Meggie is not only mad, but also hurt at Colin's harsh words. She's silent all the way home as she shuffles along behind the rest of us, trying to keep her feet inside her shoes. Yeah, I know I wasn't very supportive with the cop thing, but what could I do without getting myself in trouble?

When we return, Meggie goes to her room, but I go to the Gilmores'. Colin brings out soft drinks, and the three of us settle onto the couches.

"The sun gave me a headache," Colin says.

"Take it for a headache or a heartache," Jennifer says, imitating the commercial, and tosses a Lotus pill to her brother. Then she turns to me. "Want one, David?"

For the first time I consider it. What harm could one pill do? The way people are popping them right and left, they're obviously not that strong. They're not illegal, and they make you feel good. Mom and Gramps won't be home for another hour, so . . .

"Sure, why not?" I find myself saying. "Just one."

"All right!" Colin says with a big grin as Jennifer unwraps the pill and pops it into my mouth.

It has a sweet taste, and it's a bit chewy, like caramel, but they tell me I have to swallow it to get the full effect. I swallow.

"Since it's your first time, you're really gonna feel it," Jennifer tells me. "We need to have a couple to feel anything."

"Yeah, Jennifer," Colin says. "Throw me another."

I expect to get slaphappy and loopy—you know, like the guys from *Dumb and Dumber*—but I don't. I just get really, really relaxed.

"I was supposed to go to the store today," I say lazily, "but you know what? I'm sick of doing what I'm supposed to do all the time. Besides, I'm sure we have enough food to last one more day."

I am fixated on one spot—Jennifer's left earlobe.

"That's the most beautiful ear I've ever seen," I tell her. She and Colin crack up.

But this is really serious. Somebody—maybe Gramps—should do a painting of that ear. It would become as famous as the *Mona Lisa*.

"Everything's beautiful when you're in Lotus land," Colin says.

"I know what you mean, jelly bean," I come back.

They crack up again.

"What's a jelly bean?" asks Jennifer.

"Never mind. Not important. Don't sweat it. Let's pake a bizza," I say. "I mean . . . bake a pizza."

"You're speaking nonsense," Colin says.

"Oh, I forgot," I mutter. "This place is so bass-ackwards, you don't even know what a pizza is."

They don't smile at that.

"Maybe you'll inform us," Jennifer says coolly.

I'm suddenly very irritated, and I don't even want to deal with anybody so ignorant that they don't know what pizza and jelly beans are.

I manage to get to my feet; I wobble around a bit, then say with a sneer, "Behold your typical Fashion City teenagers!"

When I go into our apartment, Meggie is still in her room. I slip into my own room and fall across the bed in a daze. I hear Mom and Gramps come in, but nobody disturbs me. I drift away to the sound of their voices in the kitchen. The next thing I know, Gramps is knocking on my door.

"Dinner, David. Come and eat."

At the table I'm quiet. I wonder if my pupils are dilated. I try not to meet anybody's eyes. Meggie starts telling Mom and Gramps about the cop taking her shoelaces, and they become absorbed in her story.

"Not to worry, sweetie," Mom says to Meggie. "I have an extra pair for you."

"But Kitty picked out those shoelaces for me," Meggie says. "They can't be replaced."

Gramps speaks up. "Meggie B., I promise to buy you the gaudiest, brightest-colored shoelaces in the universe when we get out of this place."

It's disgusting how they treat her. Like she's the little princess.

"Is something wrong, David?" Mom says to me.

"No. Why do you ask, Mother dear?"

"I don't know. You don't seem like yourself."

"Who else would I be?"

Meggie is eyeing me. Does she know? Yeah, maybe little baby girl knows. But she won't tell. The moment passes, and I think I'm home free.

Then Mom says, "David, last night before we went to bed, I reminded you to get milk, and now I see there's none in the refrigerator."

"Oh, the milk," I say. "I guess I forgot."

"Did you go to the store at all?"

I shake my head.

"We don't have a thing for breakfast," she says irritably. "We're also out of fruit. Did you waste the whole day?"

I shrug and avoid her eyes.

"David, I don't ask much of you, but—"

"All right! All right!" I cry, and jump up from the table. "I'll go! Just get a grip, will ya?"

I can see the shock on Mom's face, and Meggie's eyes go wide.

"Apologize to your mother," Gramps says to me, his face and his tone, for once, stern and serious.

"Sorry," I mumble. "I'll go now."

"But they'll soon be closing," Mom says, "and—"

I bolt out the door without a backward glance, before she can finish her sentence.

One Lotus for a difference you'll notice? I notice, all right, but it's not the kind of difference I expected. There's a nice breeze outside, and I think my head might clear up. In front of the other buildings, young kids are playing on the sidewalks, trying to catch the last bit of daylight.

I suddenly remember that I left my cap in my room. I have a vial of vinegar in my pocket, but that's no good when you can't see your head. I consider going back for it, but the store closes at eight. I have to hurry and hope for the best.

I'm passing Building 4 at a trot when I happen upon a kid about ten years old sitting by himself on the curb. He's mumbling something, and I pause beside him to eavesdrop.

"Conformity is contentment," he's saying. "The daydreamer is discontented."

He repeats both sentences over and over. Gross reiteration again. It must be even more common than gross vacillation.

I move on, thinking of Meggie and Alison Fink that day in the clothing store. Alison did seem happier after Meggie talked to her. Yeah, sometimes Meggie just accidentally does the smart thing.

At the market, I have to rush to find the things we need. The overhead lights begin to blink, indicating closing time, and I hurry to the register to pay for my groceries.

On the way home I'm surprised to find the boy still sitting there on the curb by himself reiterating the same phrases.

I listen to him for a moment, then sit down beside him, placing the groceries at my feet. Maybe I'll give it a try.

"Got a nice little song for you," I tell the boy. "I'm going to say it like a poem. It's about wolves, see? Bet you didn't know they used to roam the planet, happy and free as the wind. Here's what they would say if we could hear them today: 'I remember moonless nights across the frozen land. . . .'"

The boy says nothing. His face is expressionless, and he keeps saying his mottoes in a weary monotone.

"Conformity is contentment. The daydreamer is discontented."

" 'I remember cold blue nights of ice and wind,'" I say to the kid. "Can't you just see those wolves in the moonlight? That's a nice picture you can daydream on. What's your name?"

"Conformity is contentment. The daydreamer is discontented."

"Their contentment came from living in harmony with the land," I say, continuing my wolf story.

He looks at me, and I'm encouraged, so I go on. " 'Once the wolves were here. Wild hearts without fear.'"

"Conformity is contentment. The daydreamer is discontented."

" 'Wild hearts without fear!' " I say again. "Can you say that?"

"Conformity is contentment. The daydreamer is discontented."

Man, if I had to live with that constant reiteration day in and day out, it would drive me nuts. It's really infuriating.

"I bet your mom doesn't like to hear that all the time,

does she?" I ask him. "You should surprise her by saying something different tonight."

"Conformity is con—"

"Come on, kid, it's not that hard," I say. I'm about to lose it. "Say 'Wild—'"

And that's when I see a single teardrop sliding down his cheek. Bummer.

"Hey, dude, don't cry," I say. "It's okay."

"Jeremy!" a voice calls, and the kid's head turns to face the building. In the approaching darkness, I can make out the shape of a woman standing on a balcony on the second floor. "Come in now, Jeremy," she calls.

The boy leaps to his feet and bolts toward the door of Building 4. With hands on hips the woman stands there watching me. I notice then that all the kids have gone in. It must be close to eight-thirty. I stand up, grab my sack of groceries, and hurry toward Building 9. I am passing Building 6 when I hear someone yelling the word that chills me to the bone.

"Lockdown!"

· 24 ·

I take off at a gallop.

Building 7. What happens when you don't make curfew? I don't know, and I don't want to find out. I run faster.

Building 8. I can hear all the television sets in the city coming on at the same time: "Welcome to *The Family Hour.*"

Building 9. Surely Tom will see me coming and let me in. I grab the front-door handle. Locked. I pound on the door. Tom doesn't appear. He must have locked himself in already. Panic.

If a night watchman comes along, will he—*can* he—let me in? Will I be arrested and taken to the police station? Will they do a mug shot of me for *The Family Hour*?

"Thirteen-year-old David Blue of Sector B," I can imagine Sherry Cross reporting, "was arrested for missing curfew last night. He will be taken before a firing squad at dawn and executed."

Now it's dark, and from inside the building I can hear *The Family Hour* blasting out its message to the robots of Fashion City. Mom must be out of her mind with worry. What to do? I count six floors up, then two balconies over. Or three? Which one is ours? I'm not sure.

I check a side entrance, which is also locked, then walk around to a rear door—also locked. I slump beside an air-conditioning unit under a first-floor window and stay there, trying to clear my muddled brain. After a while I hear voices coming from the front of the building. Two men are talking. Maybe night watchmen? Should I approach them or stay hidden?

The men seem to be coming around the corner of the building. I press myself against the wall and watch the place where they will soon appear, but they stop just before the corner. At this point I can hear their conversation.

"So, tell me, Carl," the first man says, "what's the job you're training me for?"

"They didn't tell you?"

"No, they just told me to report tonight. Said they needed somebody right away."

"We're bounty hunters," Carl explains. "We catch curfew breakers."

"What if it's just some poor creep who's on his way to the night shift and runs out of time?" says the first guy.

"Tough luck. You know the law, Kevin. They have to be locked in by eight-thirty whether they're at home or on the job."

"Do you catch a lot?" asks Kevin.

"On my best night I caught three. A few times I caught two. About once a week I catch one. But most nights? None. That's how it goes."

"And what do you do with them?"

"Haul 'em down to the police station. That's where you get paid."

"And what do the police do?"

"They do a harsh interrogation," Carl replies, "trying to find out if they're gross agitators or just unlucky enough to miss curfew."

"How are they punished?" asks Kevin.

"Depends on what the police find out in the interrogation. Could be just a warning, could be rehab, or could be—you know, the ultimate."

The ultimate? These words hang in the air. I can hear my own heart beating. Would they give the ultimate to a thirteen-year-old boy?

If Kevin and Carl walk about ten steps around that corner, they'll see me huddled against the building. The AC unit clicks on and makes a loud humming noise so that I can no longer hear what they are saying.

My eyes search the darkness. Maybe I'll hide behind another AC unit—one that's farther away from these bounty hunters. Then I realize I'm clutching the bag of groceries tightly against my chest. I need to ditch it. I carefully set the bag down on the ground, glance toward the corner of the building to make sure the men aren't in sight, and then make a dash for a distant AC unit. I find a silent one, curl up behind it, and pull my knees under my chin. I know I'm just barely hidden, but it's pretty dark out here.

Soon I hear the voices again, and I can tell they're coming my way.

"Look at this. Somebody left groceries on the ground," Kevin says. "Milk, fruit, and . . . I'll bet there's a mad mom somewhere in there tonight."

Mom. The word stabs my heart. Mom. Gramps. Meggie. They're probably up there pacing the floor during *The Family Hour.* Is Meggie crying? Probably. I tighten my grip around my legs and pull my knees closer to my chin. How long can I stay in this position? Already I'm beginning to cramp. But the bounty hunters are still there. In fact, now they're only a few feet from me, and it seems they're in no hurry to leave.

As I realize I can't sustain this position much longer, fear begins to move through me like a slow hot wave of lava. Now I'm sure the Lotus has worn off. I think again of Meggie. She must have felt like this when the madman threatened her. And when she woke up all those nights screaming. So much fear for a little girl.

At that moment, Kevin says, "Hey, man, look at that!"

"Look at what?" Carl comes back.

"That blue light over there," Kevin says. "It's fluorescent."

Blue fluorescent light? No, no, not now!

"You mean that glow behind the AC unit over there?" Carl says. "Yeah, man, I see it. Let's check it out."

· 25 ·

Back to Meggie

"Something must have happened to him," Mom tells Tom when he comes for lockdown and David has not returned from the store. "He wouldn't miss curfew. He has nowhere to go." She stands there in the doorway, refusing to move out of Tom's way. "Just give him a few more minutes," she pleads.

"You know what?" Tom says. "When somebody gets sick or hurt, the police take 'em to the clinic. So I'll call there for you if you like."

"Please, would you?"

"Sure. Now go on inside and let me lock up. It's the rules."

Reluctantly Mom moves, and Tom quickly locks us in. At the same time, *The Family Hour* comes on. Mom covers her ears with her hands. Gramps puts an arm around her, and she rests her head on his shoulder.

"We've got to get out of this place," she mumbles.

"There may be something about David on *The Family Hour*," Gramps says.

The three of us sit down on one couch to watch.

Sherry Cross is beaming. "A night for celebration, good people of Fashion City," she says. "There were no arrests today."

I slump against the cushions.

"In other news," Sherry Cross continues, "at least five children who are afflicted with gross reiteration have caught a very strange virus. They've been heard repeating this nonsensical phrase."

The camera pans across five kids of various ages, and they are reiterating something oh so familiar: "It's not easy being green."

I catch my breath sharply.

"Where they picked it up," Sherry Cross continues, "and what it means, nobody seems to know. The clinic staff has not determined how this virus should be treated."

So Kermit's words must have worked for Alison, and now she has taught them to others. You go, girl! I glance at Mom and Gramps, but I can see that their minds are far away from what's on TV. Later I'll confess all, but now is not the time.

The phone rings, and it's Tom reporting that David is not at the clinic.

"Do you have a number for the police?" Mom says frantically. Then she says no more. In another moment she hangs up and sits back down between me and Gramps.

"We're not allowed to call the police," she says, "unless we have a crime to report."

Normally I would cry at this point, but not tonight. No, I won't cry. Mom needs me to stay calm. We sit through the rest of *The Family Hour*, lost in our own fears and terrible imaginings.

"Thirty minutes until lights-out," Sherry Cross says brightly. "Sleep well, happy people of Fashion City."

"Sleep well?" Mom says to the TV. "You know what, Sherry Cross? You really suck!"

I am so startled and tickled at Mom's words, I'm afraid I'm going to be hysterical. I choke and catch Gramps's eye. He looks away quickly. Any other time we would be howling over this.

At ten we meet the Gilmores on the balcony as usual. When Mom breaks the news about David, Jennifer begins to cry.

"I gave him a Lotus," she sobs.

"What!" Mom cries.

Jennifer nods. "I'm sorry. I should have let you know, so you could watch out for him."

"He'll survive," Colin says coldly.

"That explains his behavior at dinner," Gramps says.

"What will the police do to him?" Mom asks.

"They'll knock him around a bit," Colin says, "then let him go."

"What do you mean 'knock him around'?" Mom says.

"Enough, Colin," Gil says to his son, then turns to Mom. "They'll probably just give him a warning, and that will be the end of it unless he gets caught again."

Nothing else is said about David, or about anything else, for that matter. Mom stands and peers over the balcony railing as if she's expecting to see David down there. Silence lies thick like a blanket over us. In a little while Gramps suggests in a whisper that we call it a night, and nobody gives him an argument. Colin braces his feet against the railing and pulls himself up through the trapdoor; then he gives Jennifer a hand.

"Please don't worry," Gil says to Mom, "and try to get some sleep."

But she goes inside without a word to him. Gramps and I say good night to Gil and follow Mom inside.

All night I feel Mom tossing and turning beside me. Several times she gets up and walks through the dark apartment.

At one point I hear her whispering to Gramps in the hallway.

" 'Knock him around'? What does that mean? I feel so helpless. There's nobody to call or to listen. In this place it seems nobody cares about anybody else."

I can hear Gramps murmuring comforting words.

Finally I fall into a nightmarish dream of our first day in Fashion City.

"The Fathers take care of the people."

"You'll like it here. Everybody does."

· 26 ·

David Speaks

"Well, what have we here?" one of the men says with a chuckle, and I recognize the voice as Carl's.

The two of them haul me out from behind the AC unit to a standing position. My legs are trembling so that I can hardly keep them from buckling.

"What's on your head, boy?"

"P-paint," I stutter. "J-just paint."

"I never saw no paint like that. Did you, Kevin?"

"No, I never did. It's shining all over the place. You from another planet, kid?"

These words send shock waves through me, but Carl and Kevin are laughing their heads off.

"Honest," I say, "it's just paint."

"Whatchu been paintin', kid?"

"Uh . . . well, this friend of my mom's, he works as a

sign painter. He paints those signs down there by the river."

"What signs?" Carl says.

My mouth is so dry, my lips are sticking to my teeth. "You know the ones. No Swimming. No Fishing. You know?"

"Yeah, I've seen those signs," Kevin says. "So what?"

"Well, I was helping my m-mom's friend, and I got some in my hair, that's all."

"What's his name? Your mom's friend?"

"I d-don't know. I mean, I forgot."

"You're lighting up the city," Carl says.

"It's fluorescent paint," I say. "It's supposed to glow in the dark."

For a long, miserable moment I stand there under their scrutiny. My own light casts a blue halo over their faces, and I can see their bewilderment. Anybody with a brain would know that even fluorescent paint wouldn't glow this brightly. So I pray they don't have brains.

"I never saw anything like it," Carl mutters.

"Me neither" comes from Kevin.

I try to divert their attention from my hair by saying, "I missed c-curfew, and I was scared. So I hid."

Still they continue to stare at me.

"Can you let me into my building?"

"Not on your life, boy. We'll collect a reward for you down at the police station."

"Please, just let me in. My family will give you a reward."

They laugh again. "You're funny, kid."

"We couldn't let you in if we wanted to," Carl says. "Nobody gets in after eight-thirty. Besides, don't have no keys."

"Those your groceries back there?" Kevin asks me.

"Yeah. I just went to the store for my mom and lost track of time. Is that a crime?"

"Yes, it is," Carl says in a hard, cold voice. "Now hold out your wrists."

As if in a dream—or a nightmare—I hold out my wrists and watch Carl snap handcuffs around them.

"What's your name?" Carl asks me.

"Aren't you going to read me my rights?" I know it's a stupid thing to say even before the words are out of my mouth.

"Read you what?"

"Nothing."

"So, again, what's your name?"

"David Blue. I live with my mom, my gramps, and my sister in number 603 here in Building 9."

"Okay, David Blue Hair, let's go to the police station."

The two men kinda shove me down the alley behind Building 9. My teeth begin to chatter as I stumble along between them.

"Please just let me talk to the night watchman," I beg. "I'm sure he'll let me in just this once."

"Are you that dumb, kid?" Carl say. "There's no night watchman."

"Sure there is. I've seen him down there patrolling after lockdown."

"That was me," Carl says. "And I wasn't patrolling.

I'm a bounty hunter, and I was looking for idiots like you who can't tell time."

If it were Meggie, she would cry. If it were Meggie, she would have nightmares for the rest of her life. But it's me. It's Meggie's big brother, always so smart, so cool, and never afraid.

"What will happen to me?"

"Maybe you'll be sent away—indefinitely," Kevin says in a creepy whisper. "You know what that means?"

At the moment I don't want to know.

It takes hours and hours to get to the police station on foot. At least it seems that way. The building is so brightly lit, it looks like a huge chandelier in the middle of this dark city. Good. My hair won't look so alien under an electric light.

As we enter the front door, I think of Officer Brent. Maybe he'll be here, and maybe he'll vouch for me, tell them I'm a good kid, just new in Fashion City and ignorant of all the rules. Yeah, then he'll take me home.

But it's not Officer Brent at the front desk. It's a black man with the worst case of bloodshot eyes I've ever seen, and a scowl on his face to match. There's a nameplate on his desk that says BOB SPINDELL.

"Look, he's not glowing as much now," Kevin says to Carl.

"You should see his hair in the dark," Carl says to Bob Spindell. "It practically lighted our path."

"Who are you?" Bob Spindell growls at me.

"Is Officer Brent here?" I ask, and the sound comes out as a squeak and a croak.

"Officer Brent?" he scoffs. "Officer Brent? Boy, don't you know anything?"

"Not much," I say miserably.

"Well, Officer Brent is a white man, right?"

"Yes, s-sir."

"Blacks got the night shift. Whites got the day shift."

"Why?"

"Why?" he yells at me. "Why? I'll tell you why! 'Cause they're white, that's why! And we're black! That's why. Anything else you wanna know?"

Somewhere during this conversation, Carl and Kevin leave, probably to collect their reward in one of the other rooms, and I'm alone with this wild man. I give Officer Spindell my name, Mom's name, and our sector letter and building number.

"What's that on your head?"

"P-paint, s-sir."

"Paint?"

"Yes, sir."

Then I have to go through the story again about painting the signs.

"Please let me call my mom," I beg. "She'll be so worried."

He just looks at me and yells, *"Singer!"*

I nearly jump out of my skin at the loud boom of his voice.

A huge black man with muscles like truck tires comes lumbering down the hall. He's scary and mean-looking.

"Got one for you," Officer Spindell says to the man.

The big man says nothing, just glares at me.

"Singer's specialty is getting answers out of people," Officer Spindell says to me, "and he's real good at it." Then he gives me a big toothy grin. "So this is my advice to you—give him the answers he wants, else you might find yourself just another splatter on the wall."

"Follow me" is all Singer says.

And I do as I'm told, thinking this could be a nightmare worse than any Meggie ever had. I follow Singer to a room with a table and two chairs in it, another door to the left, a large clock on the wall, and nothing more. It's five minutes after ten. Mom and Gramps and Meggie will be meeting the Gilmores on the balcony about now. Maybe Gil will tell Mom he has a friend who knows the chief of police or somebody, and he'll just make a call, and . . . Who am I kidding?

In this room the walls might have been painted white a century ago, but now they are pretty well messed-up with rust-colored stains. Rust-colored stains? I think of what Spindell said about splatters on the wall. Was he serious? Could those stains be dried blood? I swallow hard.

"Sit down," Singer commands.

I collapse into one of the chairs. Singer sits down heavily in the other one and lets out a long, slow sigh.

"What's that in your hair?"

It comes to me that if I could get rid of the blue, maybe it would be forgotten.

"It's paint," I say, "and I've got some paint thinner right here in my pocket. Can I get it?" I indicate my right pocket with my cuffed hands.

"You've got paint thinner in your pocket?"

"Yeah, in a vial. I've been helping this man paint signs, and sometimes I get it all over me. Can you . . ." I lift my hands to remind him that I'm cuffed.

Singer stares at me until I feel like a worm. Oh, if only I could crawl away and out of his sight.

"I just want to p-prove to you it really is p-paint," I stammer. "So you won't think it's s-something else."

"What else would it be?" he asks.

I have no answer for that, and I expect he'll push me for one, but what can I say? Then Singer surprises me by standing up and coming around the table with a key. Silently he unlocks the cuffs, then sits down again.

I pull out the vial of vinegar and open it. "Got a mirror?"

Singer rolls his eyes. "Bathroom right there," he says, indicating the other door. "Keep it open."

I go into the bathroom and look at my reflection in the mirror. My face is pale and dirty, and my eyes seem all hollowed out. With trembling fingers I apply the vinegar to the blue, and in a matter of seconds it has dissolved. Then I go back to face my fate.

"Do you work for the Resistance?" Singer says to me, and his voice comes out flat and tired.

"No, sir. I don't even know what it is."

"Who's your leader?"

"I told you I don't work for them."

He leans across the table and says, "We can do this the easy way, boy, or we can do it the hard way. Now, give me names."

Tears are forming in my eyes. I can't help it. "I swear

to you," I say with as much sincerity as I can muster. "I went to the store for my mom and lost track of time. That's why I missed curfew."

And much to my shame, the tears spill over.

"You know what I can't abide, boy?" Singer says with a sneer. "Crybabies, that's what. Ethan Singer hates crybabies."

These words remind me of all the times I have scoffed at Meggie for crying. I wipe my tears on my T-shirt and sit up straight.

"So Singer is your last name?" I ask in a calmer voice.

"I ask the questions," Singer says. "You answer them."

Still I go on. "Do you know Kitty Singer?"

Singer's eyes narrow. "How do you know Kitty?"

"She's my sister's friend."

No, no, that can't be right. Blacks and whites can't be friends here.

"I mean, they know each other, and Meggie was really upset when Kitty was arrested."

Again he looks at me for a long time, and I hold my breath. Then his face changes a little. Does it soften? He slumps slightly in his chair, and looks away toward the stained wall.

"She's my brother's little girl," he says. "Same age as my own Emma. They're like sisters. But now . . . Well, first it was my brother and his wife, and that was hard enough, but the kid?"

"Meggie cried." I speak rapidly, almost frantically, eager to relate to him on some level. "She probably had nightmares too, but she doesn't tell me about her nightmares anymore because I made fun of her. That was mean of me, and I wish I hadn't done it."

Singer is still looking at the wall.

"Meggie's a good kid," I go on doggedly, hoping for something. I don't know what. But maybe if I talk long enough, he'll forget to hit me. "And Kitty's a good kid too. She keeps you entertained. She's really funny."

Then Singer's face changes a lot. In fact, it seems to crumple right before my eyes, and for a second I think this big, tough police interrogator is going to start crying himself.

"I bet your little Emma is a cute kid." I plunge ahead. "I mean, if she's anything like Kitty, she's gotta be cute and smart and funny too."

"It ain't right," Singer says, "to send away a kid like that—for an indefinite period."

"What does that mean?" I ask in a whisper. " 'Indefinite period'?"

Finally his eyes come back to my face. He doesn't answer my question but repeats, "I tell you it ain't right."

I can't think of anything else to say right now, and I sit perfectly still while Singer goes back to staring at the wall, deep in thought.

Finally he speaks again. "It ain't right to treat kids that way."

I feel a tiny thrill of hope. I won't interrupt his thoughts.

"My old man," he says. "Her own grandpa. How could he do that?"

I stare at my hands and wait, and wait.

"I can't do this anymore," Singer finally says, and his big hands fall to his sides.

Still I don't speak. Does he mean he can't finish my interrogation? I'm afraid to ask. He continues to stare at the wall.

"I just can't do this job anymore."

Oh, the job. He can't do this job anymore. Does that mean . . . ? Long minutes go by. Then Singer stands up and looks directly at me.

"I'm giving you a warning this time," he says. "I'll tell Spindell. Now you put your head on the table and sleep, you hear me? You see that clock on the wall? As soon as it shows six o'clock, you get out of here. Nobody will stop you. Okay?"

My head bobs up and down rapidly, and Singer clumps out of the room without a backward glance. Can I be this lucky? Will he change his mind and come back? Or maybe somebody else will come in here and finish the job? I'll just rest my head here, as I was told, and be quieter than the night. Maybe they'll forget about me. If I can't sleep, I'll keep my eyes closed anyway, and pray for six o'clock.

I think of Mom and how I talked to her at dinner, how I don't help her nearly enough, what a good mother she is, how proud Dad would be of her.

Then I think of Meggie. I remember how I teased her about not achieving blue, how I haven't been an understanding brother, how I don't give her enough credit for being smart, and she really is a brainy girl.

Am I jealous of her? Do I think maybe Mom and

Gramps give her more attention than they give me? But she needs them more. She was traumatized when she was really young.

Then I think of taking the Lotus after Mom told me not to touch the stuff. What a stupid thing to do. I sleep off and on, fitfully, fearfully on that hard, cold table, and my dreams are gray, distorted, nightmarish—like the Land of the Fathers.

· 27 ·

Back to Meggie

I can hear the sound of dishes in the kitchen. Mom and Gramps are eating their breakfast. Even with David missing, they must go to work whether they like it or not. You don't get days off in this place for much of anything. Keeping the factories humming is the main purpose in life, regardless of the pain in your heart.

I don't usually get up until eight or later, but how can I sleep this morning? I roll out of bed and join them in the kitchen.

"Heard anything?" I ask, but I already know the answer.

They shake their heads and say nothing. They are eating a nuked frozen dinner for breakfast, because that's all we have. Mom's eyes are weary from anxiety and lack of sleep, and Gramps seems to have aged overnight.

We hear the front door open. We all leap to our feet and run out to see *David*!

He's filthy from head to toe, and his eyes look worse than Mom's. We fall all over him, hugging him, crying, and everybody talking at the same time.

"What happened?"

"Where have you been?"

When we give him a chance to answer, he just looks at us with big sad eyes and says, "Sorry you were worried, but I'm all right. Nobody hurt me." His voice is weird and doesn't sound like him at all. "Right now I can't talk about it."

It occurs to me that something in my brother has vanished overnight and something else has come to take its place.

"Of course," Mom says. "Go to bed and get some sleep."

"Right," Gramps says. "We have to go to work, but you can tell all tonight."

"Will you wake me for my lesson, Meg?"

"Sure, and I'll go to the store for you too."

"Don't you want something to eat?" Mom asks him.

"Not now. Maybe when I get up."

And he goes down the hallway and disappears into his bedroom.

While David rests, I go to the grocery store, then spend the rest of the morning studying the Carriage computer. I think I'm able now to figure coordinates for different places. That part of traveling by Carriage is fairly simple. The more difficult part is what Mom and Gramps are up against—finding a place to settle in this great big universe. It has to be a place where we can blend in with the natives and where the climate is reasonable. The most difficult part of all is finding a place where either English or Chromish is spoken, and such a place seems not to exist. Plan B is to find a language similar to English or Chromish, so that we can learn it easily.

When I hear David moving around, I put the computer away. I find him standing in the middle of the hallway staring at the wall.

"David?" I say softly. "You all right?"

He looks at me but doesn't seem to really see me at first. "Yeah, I was just thinking," he says at last, as his eyes begin to focus on me.

"Thinking about what?"

"About last night. I met Kitty's uncle."

"No kidding?"

We both go into the living room, and he starts telling me the story. He has just told me about being found behind the AC unit, when his face clouds over.

"I'll tell you more later," he says.

At dinner David apologizes for his behavior yesterday. Then he tells his story in a flat, unemotional voice. For the next two days he keeps to himself. He doesn't even want to see Jennifer. He says we're not to worry about him, that he's all right and just needs some time alone. No one feels much like singing without David. Gil strums his guitar in the darkness, but it takes on a sad, lonely tone.

Finally, on the third day, David joins the world again,

because this is the day that our sector has free access to Fashion City Park from nine in the morning until curfew at eight-thirty. The adults are allowed the day off from work, and the kids are excused from chores and lessons.

At the crack of dawn, when the smog still lies thick over the city, we are up, preparing a picnic basket, gathering blankets and suntan lotion, water bottles, etc. When I think of the wild and wonderful places we visited on our Earth, it seems pathetic that we're now so excited about one day at a city park.

Mom has been sewing shorts at the factory and has managed to purchase a pair for each of us to wear today. We walk to our destination with the Gilmores, who are also in shorts. Outside the entrance to the park, and pacing back and forth, we find Bonnie. Once again her affliction is creating problems for her, and again it's Jennifer who helps.

"I couldn't decide what to bring," Bonnie says plaintively. "So I didn't bring anything. I'm the only one not taking stuff to the park."

"That's okay, Bonnie," Jennifer assures her. "We've brought enough food and water and other things to share with you. You can spend the day with us."

"Oh, thank you, Jennifer!" Bonnie cries. "Thank you! You see, I just couldn't decide!"

"Bonnie's situation is unusual," Gil explains as Bonnie and Jennifer walk ahead of the rest of us. "She was bitterly angry when her brothers were killed in the war, and her protests were loud and legendary. That's why she had to be sent away to rehab so often—so many times, in fact, that she became disabled. People were surprised when she was allowed to return home again and again. Also, single women usually are not tolerated, but Bonnie, inexplicably, hasn't been forced to marry. It's rumored that she actually likes the factory work, and her skill is so exceptional that the Fathers have looked the other way in her case. They generously allow her to live in that tiny apartment next to yours."

"How big of them," Gramps mumbles.

"Yes indeed," Gil agrees.

We find a shady spot, where we spread our blankets. For the summer season, there are several birthdays in our building, including Colin's sixteenth and my twelfth. The first order of the day is to sing "Happy Birthday" to us and present us with gifts. I receive a watch from Mom, socks from David, and a T-shirt from Gramps that says *You Are My Sunshine*. It's a drab brown color, but I'm pleased to see a phrase that has nothing to do with the Fathers.

Then, as bizarre as it seems to me, we are eating birthday cake in the middle of the morning. When the smog burns away, we find ourselves enjoying a shimmering summer day, and somebody organizes races, including sack and three-legged races. Mom, Gramps, David, and I enter each event and have so much fun, you might think we were in our own backyard at the old Fischer place.

For lunch we enjoy hot dogs, hamburgers, fried chicken, and desserts. And there are vendors selling ice cream and sodas, even cotton candy and snow cones. After lunch, everybody rests. We sit on our blankets and listen to Gil strumming his guitar. Mom rubs suntan lotion on my arms, and I'm so content and comfortable that I want to doze off, but I shake my head to clear it. Who would waste time sleeping on a day like this?

And that's when I see *him*! He's leaning against a tree licking ice cream from a cone. He's tall and angular, with a distasteful expression on his stained face. Suddenly he stops eating, lifts his long nose, and sniffs the air like an animal detecting a scent on the wind. The shock of seeing him again sends tremors through my nervous system, and the skin around my skull tingles.

I am transfixed by the purple map of Mexico on his face when his wild eyes meet mine. I couldn't look away from him now if my life depended on it, and before I can stop myself, I clutch Gramps's arm and begin to babble frantically in Chromish. Screeching, clicking, whistling, gurgling. And I can't stop.

Of course I immediately become the center of attention. The shrillness of my voice and the language itself seem alien even to me now, and it's a sure bet that no Earthling in any universe has ever heard such a tirade of grossly unique sounds.

Then Gramps pulls me close to him and gently places a hand over my mouth to dam the flood of words. I am silenced, but my wide eyes do not leave the madman. He is now gaping at us, and I see some sort of recognition on his face.

"It's the man with the purple birthmark," I hear Mom say to Gramps.

Now I'm disappearing into a place deep inside myself where I feel hidden. It's a trick I learned the last time I saw this horrid man. It's like a state of suspended animation, an escape into the still eye of the tornado. Nothing can touch me here.

In this safe, secret place it's like I'm watching a scene that I'm no longer a part of. The man moves toward me and my family, growling like a dog. I see David rushing at the man, and yelling something about "my sister." Several people help him grab the man, and there's a rowdy scuffle, while someone else runs for help. When the police arrive in our midst, I hear the echo . . . echo . . . echo of that other day in that other world when I was first traumatized, and the long-suppressed memories wash over me.

· 28 ·

I was in my third-grade classroom in California, and my teacher, Mrs. Barton, was preparing us for the next day's field trip to the sea. She had brought in some shells, which were spread out on her desk. I was excited to be going to the sea.

Suddenly my classmates fell silent, for there was a man standing in the doorway, looking into the room and sniffing the air with his long nose.

"It's in this room," he said. "I can smell it here."

The purple stain on his face seemed to throb and deepen in color as his eyes searched our faces.

"Excuse me, sir," Mrs. Barton said to the man. "Can I help you?"

But he didn't answer her. He was moving slowly into our midst.

"It's here," he said with a wild bright gleam of madness in his dark eyes. "There's an alien here."

"Don't come any closer!" Mrs. Barton commanded.

"I've been given this great gift," he said in a dreadful voice. "So that I can sniff them out and eliminate them from our society." He took a knife from his pocket and waved it over his head. "You don't want to sway me from my mission."

My classmates began to shriek and cry. Mrs. Barton tried to place herself between us and the awful man. That was when he zeroed in on me.

"Sir!" Mrs. Barton shouted loudly at the man as she shielded me with her body. "Please leave the premises at once!"

But he knocked Mrs. Barton aside as if she were a rag doll and reached his long bony fingers toward me. I remembered the terror as only a momentary thing, for I was falling, falling like a leaf on the breeze, before entering this hidden safe place inside.

Fortunately, the man's hands never reached me, and I was pulled from the brink of some horrible fate as the school security guards appeared. I knew no more until I saw Gramps. He lifted me from the couch in the principal's office, where I lay curled up, and held me close. He smelled of freshly baked bread.

The man was taken into custody, declared insane, and locked away so that he couldn't hurt anybody. Gramps explained to me that there really were people in the universe with superreceptive senses who were able to identify aliens.

"But I've never known them to be insane or violent," he told me. "On Chroma they were revered as wise men."

One night I heard Mom saying to Gramps, "This incident has brought unwanted publicity to us. We are no longer *anonymous. Also, insane people don't stay locked up forever, and that man will get out someday. When he does, I'm afraid he'll come looking for us."*

That was when we moved across the country to North Carolina, where I was somehow able to put behind me the horror of being hunted like an animal. Only in nightmares did I fully feel my fears.

This time it appears that the madman has sniffed out and tried to attack my entire family. Still, he is my personal childhood monster who hides in the closet or under the bed. I feel he is after only me and has tracked me across two worlds.

When I come back to the present, I find Mom, Gramps, David, Bonnie, and the Gilmores hovering over me. Mom is bathing my face with a wet cloth.

"Not to worry, Meggie B.," Gramps says. "Officer Brent took him away."

"He's a weird one," Gil says, and laughs. "He claims to be an alien hunter."

"Isn't that ludicrous, Meggie?" Mom says, and tries to laugh too, but I can see the anxiety in her eyes.

I want to comfort her, to tell her I'm okay, but I can't be sure I really am okay. And Colin is looking at me with an expression I've never seen before.

"Meggie, what *were* those sounds you were making?" he asks me.

Everybody looks at me and waits for an answer. But what can I say? What can anybody say? I feel that Mom,

Gramps, and David are searching their brains for some explanation.

"Clearly she was terrified," Mom says to Colin. "Wouldn't you be if that maniac came after you?"

But Colin and Jennifer are exchanging glances that I can't interpret. What must they be thinking?

"It's bizarre how he lunged at you all like that!" Bonnie says.

"Yeah," Colin agrees. "I've seen him lots of times, hanging around town, sniffing the air, and talking crazy about aliens among us, but I've never known him to be violent."

"I have to wonder why he hasn't been apprehended before now," Gil says. "His gross uniqueness is glaringly obvious."

"Good point," Gramps says. "Why hasn't he been arrested before now?"

"For the same reason I've been given special treatment," Bonnie says. "They need him. He knows more about the sewing machines than anybody. They usually keep him well medicated, but today he was unsupervised."

"Surely he'll be sent away now," Jennifer says. "Don't you think?"

Much to my dismay, nobody can answer that question.

I don't want to ruin this day for the others, so I pretend to be all right, and I insist that they continue to participate in the activities. I'll just remain here on the blanket, I tell them, and get my bearings. Mom and Gramps, however, won't leave my side, and David stays close by. The rest of our group do manage to go back to their holiday and put aside the man with the purple birthmark, but I know he'll reappear in my dreams for many nights to come.

Several times throughout the day, I find Colin staring at me with knitted brows. When his puzzled eyes meet mine, he turns away quickly. When we finally leave the park to go back to Building 9, we see Elvis Presley performing on the sidewalk again.

As we stop to listen to his music, Gramps whispers to me, "It really is Elvis."

Yes, it really is, and apparently he's back from rehab, but not in all his glory. Gone are the shiny, silky clothes and blue suede shoes. Now he's dressed in beige from head to toe, and his dark wavy hair has been mutilated into a crew cut. Worse yet, all the light has gone out of his eyes, and he doesn't allow his body to sway in the least. Worst of all, he sings that most bland of all love songs, "Tea for Two."

I think of the other Elvis, and the contrast makes me long for those sparkling golden days in America. Not just the green mountains and valleys, and blue waters, but also the happy people who were in charge of their own destiny. The energy. The wild music. The spirited laughter. The freedom from fear. And my heart aches to see that Earth again.

· 29 ·

On *The Family Hour* we hear that the madman has been sent away for "an indefinite period of time," but now I have a hard time trusting anybody or believing anything I hear in this place, and a new phobia creeps into my mind. I'm afraid of going outside, even for a walk. My family is patient with me, but Jennifer and Colin simply don't get it.

"You need fresh air and sunshine," Jennifer tells me. "A strong body serves the Fathers far better than a weak one."

I can't help thinking that I really have not breathed fresh air since coming to Fashion City. In fact, it's likely that the air-conditioning is safer than the polluted air outside. Mom has told me that it's only a matter of time before the lifelong residents here begin to come down with pollution poisoning, as they did on Chroma.

This morning Mom told us she has found what she thinks is a promising planet. Its name is Tranquility, its language is very much like Chromish, and it has strict environmental regulations. Now she and Gramps have to study the various governments to see if they can find a place like the United States.

I wonder how the Gilmores will take it when they wake up one morning and find that the Blues have vanished overnight. I'll miss them, but we knew this day was coming.

Later we're sitting on the balcony on a night so dark you can't see your hand in front of your face. No moon, no stars. It seems that Mom's refusal to marry Gil has only made him more in love with her, and he keeps asking her, "How can I win your heart? What must I do?" Mom has tried patiently to explain to him that her heart can't be won, but on this night she tries a different tactic.

"You can give up those stupid pills, for one thing," she snaps at him.

Gil is obviously surprised. "Give up Lotus? But why?"

"They take all the natural survival instinct out of you, Gil, and make you sluggish."

"But they make life bearable. You should try them yourself, my dear. David had a bad reaction. They usually make you more agreeable."

"Oh, yes, I'm sure of it," Mom replies with a laugh, "more agreeable and more submissive. That's how they turn you into zombies."

"Meggie!" This cry from Colin is sudden and shrill. "What's in your hair?"

Once again, all eyes are on me, and from the corner of my right eye, I can see why. OMG! I am glowing!

"What on earth . . . ?" Gil says.

"It looks like about a hundred fireflies!" Jennifer screeches. "Or a thousand!"

"Yeah, blue fireflies," Gil says, "nesting in your hair!"

"And it just gets brighter and brighter!" Colin adds.

This cannot be explained away as paint, and we all know it. On this dark night I'm beginning to light up the balcony with what must look like a periwinkle fluorescent bulb attached to the right side of my head. I am so excited, my teeth start to chatter.

"Come, Meggie," Mom says calmly. "Let's go inside and have a look." Once inside, she whispers, "It's the loveliest shade of blue I've ever seen."

She hugs me, and now I can't stop grinning. Yes! I have finally achieved blue.

"Too bad we have to wipe it out," she says as I follow her into the kitchen.

I am lighting the way, so Mom finds the vinegar quickly and cleans the luminescent stripe with a paper towel.

"What will we tell the Gilmores?" I whisper.

"Nothing," Mom says. "Don't worry about it."

"But what if they tell somebody?"

"And have people consider them as loony as the madman?" Mom says with a chuckle. "Besides, we'll be gone from here soon."

As we approach the glass doors, which we left open, I can hear Gil saying, "I don't understand. What *was* that?"

"What was what?" Gramps says.

"You know exactly what," Gil says. "That blue light. What the heck was it?"

"Blue light? I didn't see any blue light. Did you, David?"

"Nope," David comes back. "Maybe you guys are taking too many blue pills."

"Oh, come on. Don't give me that," Colin says. "What's wrong with Meggie?"

"Nothing's wrong with our Meggie!" Gramps says loudly and with much feeling.

"But the way she was jabbering in the park the other day," Colin goes on, "like she was having some kind of fit. And the way her hair lit up. Is she sick?"

"Stop it, Colin!" Gil scolds him.

"I'm just saying," Colin goes on, "if you're trying to protect her from being sent away, we're not going to turn her in."

"We'd never do that," Jennifer adds.

Mom and I resume our places on the porch.

"I don't know what to tell you, Colin," Mom says, "but no, Meggie is not sick."

"Then what?" Colin persists. "I mean, that's not normal!"

"Yes! Yes, it *is* normal!" Gramps says emphatically. "And that's all we can tell you."

"But we've never seen anything like this," Colin says. "She's spooky."

I am suddenly so mad at him, I can't see straight.

"Yeah, maybe I am spooky," I cry. "But at least I don't pretend not to see when a policeman bullies somebody, and I don't yell at people to shut up!"

I didn't mean to say that, but I realize now it's been bothering me for days, and I'm glad it came out.

"And you, kiddo, are grossly unique," Colin fires back.

"Thank you!" I cry out with a laugh in my voice. "That's the nicest thing anybody's said to me since I've been in this place."

"It wasn't meant as a compliment," Colin mumbles.

"Colin! Not another word from you!" That's Gil putting his foot down.

After a short silence, Colin whispers, "I hope the night watchman didn't see her."

"What night watchman?" David speaks up. "You really think there's somebody down there looking out for us? Well, think again. There's only bounty hunters."

It's for sure, our friends now see us in a new light, so to speak, and it seems even more essential to leave this place quickly.

At breakfast Gramps says, "We'll set up the Carriage this evening."

"So you've settled on Tranquility?" David says excitedly.

"Yes," Mom says. "It has its problems, like every place, but we need to get away—yesterday!"

"It'll take twenty-four hours for the Carriage walls to restore," Gramps explains. "Then we'll be ready to leave the Land of the Fathers forever."

"Amen!" Mom says with a long sigh. "We have only today and tomorrow to work in that stinking factory. Maybe I can stand it for that long."

Poor Mom. She has tried to hide her frustration with the monotony of her work, but now she doesn't have to do that anymore.

That afternoon the telephone rings, and I'm reminded of our second day in Fashion City, when Joe installed it. We've been here for the entire summer season now—autumn is upon us—and the phone has rung only a few times. Though Mom and Gramps have made calls on occasion, David and I haven't used it at all.

"Hey," Jennifer says when I answer. "There's something I've been curious about. How come your mom was fussing at my dad for taking Lotus?"

"Because she thinks it's addictive, Jennifer. You all may be addicted already."

"The Fathers have us watched for symptoms of Lotus abuse," Jennifer explains. "That's one of Tom's jobs. He knows all the signs, and reports when he sees them. Then you're called in for rehab. They don't want anybody so out of it we can't function."

"But why take Lotus at all?" I say.

"Because it makes you feel good."

"When it comes to feeling good," I tell her, "I always listen to Gramps's advice. He says he never feels bad, and he's the healthiest person I know."

"Yeah, for an old person he seems to have a lot of energy," Jennifer agrees. "Exactly what is his advice?"

"Just the basics," I explain. "Eat right and exercise."

"How old is Gramps, anyway?"

I laugh. "Well, he tells everybody he's sixty, but he's really sixty-five."

"No!" Jennifer screams suddenly into my ear. "No! Stop it!"

"What are you talking about?"

But Jennifer has hung up. A moment later she's banging on our door.

"Now they know!" she cries frantically. "And they'll come for him."

"What do you mean, Jennifer?"

"They know how old Gramps is, and they'll force him into Vacation 65."

"How would they know?"

"The phones are bugged!"

"What! There's a tap on our phone?"

"On everybody's," Jennifer says as her pretty face melts into gloom. "The Fathers are fond of reminding us that we have privacy inside our homes. And it's true. We do. But what good is it when the phones are bugged?"

"That's unconstitutional!" I protest. "It's an invasion of privacy."

Jennifer stares at me, uncomprehending. Unconstitutional? Yeah, right! In this upside-down world, there is no U.S. Constitution! The Fathers make all the rules, and they make them to suit their own purposes.

"Why didn't you warn me about the phones?" I raise my voice to Jennifer.

"I keep forgetting that you don't know all the ways of the Fathers," she says miserably.

Jeez! The last thing Gramps needs right now, when we're so close to leaving this place, is a vacation. It seems to me a person should have a choice about a thing like that, but just before five o'clock, two police officers show up at our door. Boldly they walk inside and park themselves on one of our couches. I have told David about the phone call, and now we look at each other with worried eyes. I know we are thinking the same thing: we should warn Gramps.

David eases toward the door, saying, "I have to do some shopping for dinner."

"Not now," one of the officers says firmly. "Sit down. Both of you need to stay right here until the old man comes home."

As soon as Mom and Gramps walk in the door, the officers stand up, and one of them says, "Time for Vacation 65, old-timer."

"What're you talking about?" Gramps exclaims.

"The next white bus leaves the day after tomorrow. We'll hold you in custody until then—just for safe-keeping."

"I can't go on vacation now. My family needs me. Besides, I'm only sixty years old!"

The officers look at each other and laugh.

Gramps gives up way too easily. "So I lied," he admits, "but how'd you find out?"

I cringe in dread, waiting for the officer to tell on me, but he simply says, "I have no idea. We're just following orders."

On top of being mad at Jennifer for not telling me about the tap, I'm also mad at myself for giving Gramps's secret away. Mom is so distraught the night after he's taken, she actually allows Gil to put his arms around her.

"Not to worry," he explains to her. "Vacation 65 is a gift from the Fathers to the people. You stay in a luxury hotel on the oceanfront in a warm climate with everything your heart could desire, right at your fingertips. There's entertainment and fine food and festive clothing, friends of the same age, games, exercise, dancing, cruise ships. Everything you've always wanted but didn't have money or time for. Vacation 65 guests are also given the best medical care in the best hospitals and are treated like royalty."

He sounds for all the world like an infomercial.

"That's fine," Mom says, "but for how long? Even Tom couldn't tell me how long my father will be kept from us."

She's thinking of the Carriage to be set up and our upcoming voyage, and the fact that she'll have to work at that awful job until Gramps comes back.

"How long?" Gil says. "An indefinite period of time."

"Indefinite period?" David screeches.

"How long is indefinite?" Mom says irritably, and moves away from him.

"You people are obsessed with time!" Gil says tersely.

"And you people *ignore* time!" she snaps back.

On the morning of Gramps's departure, I force myself to leave our apartment and stand on the sidewalk with David, Colin, and Jennifer to watch for the white bus marked VACATION 65 to come rolling by. When we see it, we wave frantically and call to him. "Goodbye, Gramps!"

His balding head appears at one of the windows, and I'm glad to see that he's smiling. We wave until the bus is out of sight.

· 30 ·

"Okay, the truth, Mrs. Blue." Tom speaks irritably to Mom that night because she keeps bugging him about Gramps. "He won't be coming back at all. Nobody comes back from Vacation 65, nor do they want to. They love it."

"But they can come back for visits, can't they?" David asks.

"Oh, no, that wouldn't be practical," Tom says. "It's too far away."

"How far is it?"

"I . . . I'm not real sure," Tom says, and scratches his head. "I don't think I ever heard anybody say."

Then he closes the door in our faces and locks it. Mom, David, and I stand looking at each other, too stunned to move or speak. Never coming back. *Never?* We'll never see Gramps again?

As *The Family Hour* comes on, Mom sinks onto the

couch and covers her ears. David and I sit on either side of her. I try very hard to stop the flow of tears, but I can't. Then I feel Mom's arm around me, and I realize that all three of us are crying. We sit huddled together, trying to comfort each other, as the white bus flashes by us on the television screen.

Sherry Cross is chirping like a songbird, "Another happy group of seniors on their merry way to Vacation 65!"

Miserably, we watch the old people, with Gramps among them, get off the bus at the grand resort. He's smiling. I'm glad of that. But he doesn't know yet, does he? No, he doesn't know. He couldn't smile if he knew he was never coming home to us again.

When it's announced at the end of the hour that we have thirty minutes until lights-out, Mom speaks up with determination in her voice.

"We have to find him and steal him away."

"But how?" I ask.

"They are taken to a place called Farlands. We have to learn where that is," Mom says. "All we need is a location, and the Carriage can find it."

"The Carriage?"

"Yes. We have to set it up now while we have lights. Come, help me."

We follow Mom to the bedroom.

"Make room for it," Mom says to us as she takes the backpack from the closet.

We understand, and begin to rearrange the room so there will be space for the Carriage when it's fully restored.

For the next half hour Mom works quietly, doggedly, giving brief, curt commands to me and David.

"Hand me that dowel."

"Snap it here."

"Take the kink out of that corner."

We obey without a word, as we know we're racing the clock. When the lights go out at ten, Mom is fitting the last dowel into its socket. The Carriage makes a soft humming sound as its walls begin slowly to rise.

Later we sit on the balcony with the Gilmores.

"I need to know where Farlands is," Mom says to Gil.

"But my dear," Gil says, "believe me when I tell you your dad is as happy as a clam. They say Vacation 65 is so wonderful that you forget everything else. At first you might miss your family, but in time you're so busy, and your life is so full, you just leave all your worries behind you."

"Don't give me that baloney!" Mom shouts at him. "Do you know where it is or not?"

All is quiet. I have rarely heard Mom raise her voice, and in the darkness, I can sense the fear beneath her angry words.

"No, I have no idea," Gil says softly. "I would tell you if I did."

"You have good reason to be upset, Mrs. Blue." Colin speaks. "I would be too, if it were my dad—and someday it will be—because Vacation 65 is not a vacation at all!"

"What do you mean?" Mom snaps at him too.

"Oh, sure, they're given *three days* of vacation," Colin

explains. "Then, on the third night, they are given a shot at bedtime. The people of the Resistance have managed to leak this information to us. Now everybody knows it, but they go on pretending. It's easier that way. So you don't have to admit that the Fathers are killing our elders."

"Stop it, Colin!" Gil commands his son.

"K-killing them?" I stammer. I almost say this in Chromish, but I muzzle myself by placing my face against Mom's shoulder.

"Yes, killing them!" Colin goes on, in spite of his dad's command, and his voice is almost as angry as Mom's. "So they won't become a burden. Just as they kill the handicapped and the seriously ill."

"Colin . . . please don't." Gil protests only mildly now, with a tremble in his voice. In the darkness, I can see him place his head in his hands.

"His bus left this morning," I say. "So this is his first night."

"That gives him about forty-eight hours to live," Colin says without emotion.

"Gil, you work for the television station," Mom says, "so you must know how I can find out where he is. Please help me."

Gil lifts his head. "Maybe I could find out," he admits, "but what good would it do? I'm telling you, it's hopeless. Don't you know that's why we swallow the pills? It's easier to take what comfort you can and live out your days in a fog—than to know what's really going on. We have learned that to fight back means an earlier death.

"You wanted to know what happened to my wife? Well, I'll tell you. She was careful not to involve me or the kids, but she was working with the Resistance, trying to undermine the Fathers. Someone—probably Tom Lincoln—turned her in, and the police took her away. We never saw her again. That's what you get for defying them."

"I understand," Mom says gently. "But suppose I told you there is hope for us? There's a way out, and I have it. We can escape and take our children to a free society."

"I wouldn't believe you."

"You said you might be able to find out where my dad is," Mom reminds him. "So if I convinced you that it's possible to escape, would you find out for me?"

"I would certainly try," he whispers.

Mom reaches over and squeezes my hand, then does the same to David.

"I have to tell," she says to us.

David and I agree. In exchange for Gil's help, we have to tell him the truth.

"We did *not* come from the Western Province" is how Mom begins to unfold our story to the Gilmores.

"I suspected as much," Gil says. "But where on earth . . . ?"

"Not from Earth," Mom says, "not originally." Then she tells them everything.

Being a teacher, my mom is thorough and descriptive in telling a story. Still, it's obvious that the Gilmores don't immediately swallow it. Far from it. Who would? But their fascination is obvious, and they listen.

Colin is the easiest to convince. "That first day we met, Meggie, you said something about a foreign language. Is that what you were doing in the park, speaking the language of your world?"

"Yes, I was speaking Chromish," I say. "It comes to me automatically when I'm upset, and it's hard to stop."

"And the blue light in your hair?" Colin goes on.

"Yeah, Meg, tell them the legacy of the lights." David's voice comes out of the darkness. "You wear the blue better than anybody."

I nearly choke. Did my big brother actually say that? I take a long, deep breath and begin our story. I manage to tell it proudly, confidently, and I realize it's the first time any of us has spoken about it to anyone outside the family.

"And that's why you call yourselves the Blues?"

"Yes, just as you are the Caucasian race, we are the Blue race."

"And the alien hunter?" Colin goes on. "He really isn't crazy?"

"Oh, sure, he's crazy," Mom says. "But . . . later, later. Right now we have urgent business." She turns to Gil. "What do you think?"

"How do you expect us to believe such a fantastic tale?" is his answer.

"David," Mom says to my brother. "Please fetch the Log."

Of course—the Log. It holds the record of our lives, and when it's played, anybody present can see the memory and feel all the sensations of the moment it was recorded, even if they weren't there. That's how it was designed to work, but some Chromians play it better than others. Mom is really good at it, but Gramps, the artiste, is better. Someday he'll teach me to play. I *know* he will.

Mom scans the Chroma years only briefly before going to America. Wheat fields, wild horses, summer rains, and sea mists appear and make themselves real to us. The Gilmores laugh and cry as they experience *almost* first-hand the beauty and bittersweetness we have captured in the Log. At midnight, to signify the end, a golden retriever nudges us with his cold nose.

Colin reaches out, trying to hold on to it. "Oh, please play it again," he whispers.

"There'll be time later," Mom tells him.

"Not for me," Colin says sadly.

"What do you mean?" Mom asks.

"My time has run out," Colin says. "I have to go to war tomorrow."

"Tomorrow!" I gasp as tears spring to my eyes. "You didn't say a word."

"I didn't want any sappy goodbyes," Colin says.

Mom speaks up. "But don't you see, Colin? Now you won't have to go!"

"How do you figure that?" Colin says, but there's hope in his voice.

"The Carriage," Mom says. "We can leave here in it."

"Will it hold us all?" Gil asks.

"It will hold two thousand pounds," Mom informs him. "And all of us together don't come close to that. We will, however, be crowded."

"But I'm scheduled to go in the morning," Colin says. "They'll come looking for me if I don't report."

"You *will* leave this place with us, son," Gil says as he places a hand on Colin's shoulder. "I promise."

"What about Gramps?" I ask.

"We still have to find out where Farlands is," Mom says.

"I know it's on a coast," Gil tells us then. "That's all I know. I don't see how I can find out more before tomorrow night."

"I know." Jennifer speaks up, and I realize she hasn't said anything all evening.

"You know?" Her dad is incredulous. "How could you possibly know?"

"Mom gave me a book before they took her away," Jennifer says in a very soft voice. "It has maps in it."

· 31 ·

David Speaks

The six of us crouch together on my bathroom floor with a burning candle. We picked this room because it has no windows and our light can't be seen. Outside, a storm has risen, and the wind shrieks like a lost spirit. Jennifer's mother's book lies open before us.

"Mom made me promise," Jennifer explains to us, "never to show this book to anyone until I felt the time was right. I didn't know what she meant then, but now I do. I think the time is right now."

Gil hugs his daughter. "You did good."

"And do you forgive me," Jennifer says to Meggie, her voice a pitiful little whisper, "for forgetting to tell you about the wiretap?"

Meggie hugs Jennifer. "There's nothing to forgive."

So everybody's hugging Jennifer. Will I ever get a turn too?

We can't all hover over the book at the same time without blotting out the candlelight, so we take turns reading aloud to each other.

The title is *Land of the Fathers*. No author is named, but it's a treasure chest of information.

"I think it was written by somebody in the Resistance," Mom says, "because it tells it like it is."

The book tells us that the Land of the Fathers is completely controlled by big-money interests.

" 'Once there was legitimate oversight,' " Gil reads.

"That means it was like America," Mom explains to the Gilmores. "There was a body of lawmakers who worked for the people."

" 'But,' " Gil reads on, " 'its leaders became corrupted with greed and betrayed the citizens. They took bribes and contributions from those who wished to influence their decisions. Gradually the people's government fell under the complete control of large corporations. Then the true role of leadership was forgotten, and the Fathers, shrewd businessmen, made the laws of the land to suit their own greedy purposes.' "

The color-coded maps show us that Fashion City stands near the spot where Missouri is located in the United States of America. The western half of the country is green and is marked as the Western Province. Fashion City borders it. That's probably why Officer Brent took it for granted that we came from there.

"Look at this purple strip down the east coast," Mom points out. "It's where the Fathers live. They have all the coastal property."

Inland from the purple strip is a brown mass representing the industrial cities. There are more than a dozen of them, each one manufacturing a different product.

The Western Province, we're informed, is a beautiful place, still partly wild, where animals roam freely and the people try to live in harmony with nature. The families build their own homes, choose their own livelihood, and coexist peacefully with the red natives of the land. Their government is a democracy, operating within the framework of a robust constitution. The powers of government are balanced among three branches.

Abraham Lincoln, Martin Luther King, Jr., and the Suquamish tribal chief Seattle hold equal positions in the executive branch. The legislative and judicial branches are similar to those in the United States.

"Sounds utopian," Mom muses out loud. "So I wonder why people escape there to come here?"

We also find that answer in the book. Fewer than two hundred people have actually returned to the Land of the Fathers in all the years since the insurrection, we read. At the beginning the returnees were the ones afflicted with a condition somewhat like gross vacillation, because they were so indoctrinated by the Fathers they couldn't adjust to the freedom in their new society. As a result, they could no longer make decisions for themselves and felt insecure without forced regimen and discipline. In more recent years there has been only a small trickle of refugees who are unhappy with the government of the Western Province.

"Malcontents, unhappy with their leaders," Mom

explains. "Even in America we had our protesters, and some of them left the country. But I'm quite sure that those people who come to the industrial cities from the Western Province, believing things will be better for them, are completely ignorant of the facts, or they have been misled in some way by outside agitators, perhaps working for the Fathers."

"The people there speak English," Meggie says.

"And they have a constitution like the one in the United States," I say.

"I'll bet they have no unnecessary wars," Colin says, "and they have animals."

"With Chief Seattle as one of the three in charge, they probably have strong environmental standards," Mom adds.

"Fill us in on Chief Seattle," says Gil.

"In our world he was a famous chief of one of the native tribes," Mom explains. "He's best known for a letter he wrote to the U.S. president regarding the relationship between the land and the people. It was quite moving. I understand there's some controversy about whether or not he actually wrote that letter, but you know what? We just might get a chance to ask him."

We all look at Mom's glowing face in the candlelight. A streak of blue is beginning to radiate at the crown of her head.

"So can we go there," Meggie whispers excitedly, "instead of going to Tranquility?"

"Yes, let's go there." Mom is also excited. "I have a

strong suspicion the Western Province is like early America. What do you think, Gil?"

Gil looks at Jennifer and Colin, then turns back to Mom. "I think we're going to trust you to make that decision. You have studied these things, and you seem to know what you're talking about."

"Look!" Meggie cries suddenly. "Down here is Farlands on this long peninsula. It's colored purple. Farlands is Florida!"

"Florida!" Mom exclaims. "So that's where he is! But in what part of Florida, I wonder?"

We find close-up maps of the tip end of Farlands. There are also photographs of buildings grouped into a large complex located near the beach. Here the official business of the Fathers is conducted. One building is marked Vacation 65, and it's the grand hotel we saw on *The Family Hour*. In spite of its fancy exterior, this building, we read, is used for all executions. The climate and the nearness of the ocean have a calming effect on the condemned, so they're less inclined to fight back.

"If we knew what room he's in," Mom says, "we could aim the Carriage for it, land beside his bed, pick him up, and take off again in a few minutes."

"Getting his room number will definitely be difficult," Gil says.

"But not impossible!" Mom declares with determination. "Nothing is impossible, if we set our minds and hearts to the task."

At the end of Mrs. Gilmore's book we find added

information written in her small, neat handwriting. It's a list of people who might help us. By each name she has added notes detailing how that person might contribute.

Lewis Jones, she has written, *is my cousin, and he works in the execution building in Farlands. Sometimes he's sympathetic to our cause. I think he can be trusted, but I'm not sure.*

"I knew Lewis when we were younger," Gil says. "I've often wondered what happened to him. So here he is with Vacation 65."

"Do you know how to contact him?" Mom says. "Perhaps he could tell you which room Gramps is in."

"I could phone him there," Gil says. "I'm allowed work-related long-distance calls from the TV station. I'll pretend to ask him something to do with work."

"Oh, could you, Gil? Would you?"

"Of course," Gil says. "But what excuse can I use for wanting to know the room number?"

"We'll think of something," Mom says in a weary voice.

It's three o'clock in the morning as we wrap up our clandestine meeting in the bathroom.

"You kids go straight to bed," Mom says.

Although exhausted, I can't sleep, and for a long time I lie awake listening. I can hear Meggie in her room, tossing and mumbling in her sleep, and Mom and Gil are whispering together in the hallway, working out details. For the first time I sense that Jennifer's dad is something more than a programmed robot. Away from Fashion City he might even turn out to be a real human being.

· 32 ·

Back to Meggie

The next morning when David and I wake up late, we find that Mom has gone to work as usual. I hurry upstairs to see Jennifer and find that Gil is gone also. Colin is nowhere to be seen.

"Did he run away," I whisper to Jennifer, "or did he go to the military?"

"Dad hid him somewhere," Jennifer also whispers. "But I don't know where."

I'm alarmed. "Suppose the police search your apartment! You know Tom would tell them we're friends, so they'll search our place too, and find the Carriage!"

"Don't worry. We've worked out a plan to prevent them from coming here. I have to call the military police at ten o'clock and put on a big act," Jennifer says. "Dad's orders."

"What kind of act?"

"I'm going to pretend to know where he's hiding and turn him in. People here rat on each other all the time, even their own family members. They're rewarded for it."

"Rewarded how?"

"In different ways. If I really turned Colin in, I could maybe get one of the jobs with the factory day care and be exempt from the military. Or I could get a bicycle, or money. Adults get things like days off from work, even automobiles if the information is considered really important."

So that would explain why Kitty's grandfather turned her in for black-market dealing. He was somehow rewarded for it.

"Bummer," I say. "But you're only pretending?"

"Of course! I truly don't know where he is, and if I did, I wouldn't tell for anything in the world."

I help Jennifer go over what she'll say to the military police, and at ten o'clock she makes the call. First she gives her name and address.

"I'm calling about my brother, Colin Gilmore," she tells them. "He was supposed to report for military duty this morning, but instead he ran off to hide, and I just happen to know where he's hiding. Can I get a bicycle for telling?" She sounds exactly like the rotten kid sister who squeals on her brother all the time.

She listens.

"Oh, you have to find him before I get my reward? Okay. Well, I know he's either on a train or on a bus. Just before he left, he told me he's been saving tokens for over a year, and I found out later he also stole *my* tokens and

Dad's. He plans to keep switching trains and buses all day long until they stop running. Then he's going to hide in whatever station he finds himself in at dark, and do the same thing tomorrow."

Jennifer pauses for her listener to speak.

"What's he going to do when he runs out of tokens? I don't know. He's not very bright. Maybe he didn't think of that."

Jennifer gives me a nervous smile; then her voice becomes whiny. "You know what that creep did to me? He took all the groceries we had in the house. Can you imagine? I don't even have anything to eat. So I hope you find him."

She pauses again.

"You betcha! Now go get him! And praise the Fathers!" She hangs up the phone and says to me, "Hopefully they'll be searching the transportation system all day." She twists her hands together nervously. "A Lotus sure would make me feel better."

"Oh, Jennifer, you don't need those things!"

"Well, it doesn't matter anyway," she says, "because Dad flushed all we had down the john, and nearly stopped it up."

"If it's yellow, let it mellow," I squeal happily, "but if it's brown, flush it down, and if it's blue, plunge it through!"

Now we are giddy with excitement. We eat breakfast together and chat about our possible future.

At one o'clock I go to my room as usual and turn on the TV to watch my class. The Carriage stands in the middle of the room, more than halfway restored. It'll be ready for flight tonight at ten o'clock. Then it occurs to me that tomorrow we'll be gone, so why bother doing my lessons? Why indeed, as David would say. I step inside the Carriage, turn on the computer, and pull up the tutorial, which I study for the next hour.

When Mom and Gil come home from work, we all meet in our apartment.

"Did you do it?" Gil says to Jennifer.

"Yes, at ten, as promised."

"And the police haven't been around?"

"No."

"She's totally good at lying," I tease. "She nearly had *me* convinced."

"Where's Colin?" Jennifer whispers.

"He's safe" is all Gil will say.

"So did you find out what room Gramps is in?" David asks.

Gil's face falls. "Wouldn't you know, this is the one day of the season when Lewis is on holiday. So I couldn't get in touch with him."

Mom collapses onto the couch. "Oh, no."

"I'm sorry," Gil says. "I did my best. I even tried to talk to somebody else there. I told him I was helping with a TV special about Vacation 65. Of course, that's not part of my job, but I was hoping that whoever was listening in didn't know any better. Anyway, the guy I talked to couldn't care less. He was grumpy and hung up on me. I was afraid to be a nuisance and draw too much attention to myself."

"But will Lewis be back to work tomorrow?" Mom asks.

"Yes, and I left a message that I would call him again in the morning."

"Well, I guess that's the best we can do," Mom says.

"I'll call early," Gil says, "and one way or another, I'll get that room number. I promise."

He sits down beside Mom and she pats his hand. "You're doing fine." Then she turns to me, David, and Jennifer. "So, kids, I'm afraid this means we can't leave tonight."

"But tonight is Gramps's second night," David says with a worried look on his face.

"I know, I know," Mom says. "And that gives us only one more night, but I don't know what else to do. Gil will get the room number tomorrow, and we can leave as soon as we get home from work. We don't have to wait until night."

"And Colin will have to stay hidden another day," Gil says.

Which will increase the danger of his being caught, we are thinking, but nobody says it. Mom will have to do that stupid job another day. But none of it can be helped.

We each pack up the few things we'll be taking with us. Timidly Gil asks Mom if he can possibly, maybe, you know, take his guitar?

And Mom replies, "Of course! How can we sing without a guitar?"

The next day Jennifer, David, and I are on pins and needles about a possible visit from the military police in search of Colin, but at five minutes before one o'clock they haven't come or called. We can only hope they're still focusing on the trains and buses.

The three of us are standing in the bedroom, admiring the Carriage, now fully restored, when David says, "Why bother with lessons today? Let's play hooky."

That's when I recall that I didn't do my schoolwork yesterday. What if . . . ?

At that moment the doorbell rings, and my heart skips a beat. Jennifer and David go out to answer the ring. I close the bedroom door and lean against it, breathlessly waiting for what I hope will not come. But it does.

David pounds on my door. "Meggie, your tutor is here!"

· 33 ·

Oh, no, no, no. The dreaded tutor.

"Come on out here where you normally do your lessons!" David calls in a very loud voice. "You know you always do your schoolwork in the living room."

I grab school supplies, and as I slip out my bedroom door, David slips in. He rolls his eyes toward the living room, then locks himself in with the Carriage.

As I enter the room, I find a man perched on one of the couches, and Jennifer has disappeared. My tutor is middle-aged, has sandy-colored hair, and is not particularly large or scary, as Tom said he would be. Still, I'll be the best girl in the world for him.

"Good afternoon, sir," I say as politely as I can.

"Call me Mr. Baum," he says grumpily. "Now, Meggie, what's the problem?"

"Problem? There's no problem, Mr. Baum. I was a bit

bored, that's all, so I didn't do my lesson yesterday. But I'm very sorry, and I'll work twice as hard today, and I promise you won't ever have to come here again."

He looks at me funny but says nothing. I sit down on the couch and turn on the TV. My class is already under way. We're doing fractions today.

"So you're bored with fractions?" Mr. Baum asks.

"Yes, sir, but I totally know my fractions. I'll show you."

"Totally?"

"Uh . . . just an expression. But I do know them."

I spend the next few minutes following my television teacher, doing everything she tells me to do, and at the same time, I illustrate fractions with a pie chart on another sheet of paper.

"No wonder you're bored," Mr. Baum says at last. "You do know this stuff."

"Yes, sir, I do."

"I understand you're new in our city, so you must have taken a placement test."

"Yes, sir, I did, but maybe I didn't feel good that day, and my mind wandered. I guess I was daydreaming."

Uh-oh. That was the wrong thing to say, because "The daydreamer is discontented," according to the Fathers.

I try to explain. "I mean, sometimes I start to think of other things. I have this whole other world in my head, you know?"

Wrong thing to say again. Mr. Baum is frowning at me.

"What I mean is my mind goes somewhere over the

rainbow, to another land." Yeah, I've got this pretty well bungled, but I manage to smile.

"I know what you mean," Mr. Baum says, and I'm so surprised I drop my pencil. "My wife, Maud, said to me the other day, 'Frank,' she said, 'are you unconscious or what?'

"And I say back to her, 'Whatever do you mean, my dear?' And she tells me that sometimes she has to speak to me three or four times to jog me out of my fantasies."

Frank? Frank Baum? No, this couldn't be *the* L. Frank Baum, the author of *The Wonderful Wizard of Oz*, could it?

"Anyway," he goes on, and laughs a little nervously, "no need to repeat what we say here today, right?"

"Right!" I agree with all my heart.

He settles back on the couch and looks out the sliding glass doors at the sky. Right now it seems he couldn't care less about tutoring. Maybe he sees his own other world out there—maybe the land of Oz.

"Uh, Mr. Baum, sir," I say to him. "Can I ask you what your first name is?"

"It's Lyman, but I don't like it. Why do you ask?"

So it must really be L. Frank Baum. Come to think of it, he looks like photos I've seen on Wikipedia, except that in those pictures he has a big mustache, and today his face is shaved clean. Maybe it's because in Fashion City, hair on the face is considered grossly unique?

"Just curious," I tell him. "Have you ever written a book?"

He looks at me sideways. "A book? I should say not. Why do you ask me that?"

"I like reading way better than arithmetic, Mr. Baum."

He hesitates for a long moment, then whispers, "I've read a few books."

"I bet you could write a real good one yourself," I tell him.

"Well, I've never tried such a thing," he says with a chuckle, and I get the feeling he is *not* telling the truth. "Why, I wouldn't know where to start."

"Can I tell you a story?" I ask him.

He fidgets around a bit but says nothing. I take that as a yes.

"It's about a little girl from Kansas, a scarecrow, a tin man, and a cowardly lion."

I can almost see his ears prick up and his eyes begin to sparkle. I start the story. Mr. Baum sits on the edge of his seat the whole time, hangs on every word, and never takes his eyes from my face. I talk for I don't know how long. I relate every detail I can remember from *The Wonderful Wizard of Oz*. When I'm finished, he asks me a thousand questions about the story. Then he sits there staring at me.

"I've dreamed such a dream as that," he says at last.

"Dreamed it?"

"Yes, I have very vivid and detailed dreams. I have seen that land many times, and I know those characters very well. I didn't have a name for Dorothy, but now I do."

"That's amazing," I say.

"It's a magnificent story," he says dreamily. "If I were

going to write a book—mind you, I said *if*—it would be something like this one."

"If you want to write it—and mind you, I said *if* too—then you should use that idea, because I don't believe anybody in *this* world has put it on paper."

He doesn't say anything, but I can almost hear his mind spinning.

"You could even add your own ideas and make it better," I tell him.

"I'm not sure it could be any better," he says, "except for one thing."

"And what's that?"

"I would name the girl Meggie instead of Dorothy. It's a more lively name. I mean, with your permission, of course."

Now I can't stop grinning. "Totally."

He walks to the sliding glass doors and once again looks dreamily into the sky. If only there were a rainbow out there right now. Wouldn't *that* be perfect? But there's nothing except haze. L. Frank Baum turns back to me.

"I do find the land of Oz interesting," he says, "very interesting indeed. But you know what is more fascinating to me? Kansas. Now, there's a place I would love to see. It seems like paradise."

Kansas? Paradise? Yeah, coming from a Fashion City person, I can see that.

Suddenly the bedroom door flies open and David comes charging down the hallway and into the living room, rubbing his eyes.

"I fell asleep," he says. "How did it go with your tutor?"

He stops dead when he sees said tutor by the glass doors. Mr. Baum is gaping in the direction of the bedroom, where David apparently has left the door standing open, giving a clear view of the Carriage.

"What is that thing?" Mr. Baum gasps. Nobody answers, and he asks, "Does it fly?"

David comes to his senses and hurriedly runs to close the bedroom door.

"The Wizard of Oz has a flying machine," Mr. Baum says. "Is that . . . ?"

David comes back and says, "It's nearly three o'clock, Meggie. I thought your lesson was over long ago."

"I guess we lost track of time," I say.

Mr. Baum is unable to contain his excitement. "I must say this has been the most fascinating tutorial I've ever had."

I turn to my brother. "David, this is Mr. L. Frank Baum."

David is rendered speechless, but it's okay, because Mr. Baum doesn't seem to notice that an introduction has been made.

"How I wish my family could meet you!" he says to me.

"Uh, well . . ." I don't know how to respond.

"*The* L. Frank Baum?" David manages to speak at last. But nobody answers him.

"I mentioned my lovely wife, Maud, to you," Mr. Baum is saying to me, "and we have four handsome boys."

"That's cool," I say.

He rubs his big hands together gleefully. "But my, oh, my, this is splendid!"

"Mr. Baum," David says. "I hope you can keep a secret."

Mr. Baum finally notices David. "Of course, my boy, I understand. I know what would be done to you and to your—your flying apparatus, and Meggie with her delightful imagination. Believe me, I *totally* know." He turns to give me a smile before going on. "And your secret is safe with me."

Still smiling, he walks back and forth across the floor several times before stopping in front of me, where I remain seated on the couch.

"I hope you'll let me come and tutor you again, Meggie, dear."

I nod, because I don't have the heart to say no.

"Wonderful, delightful, splendid," he says. "Now I must go. I have to get started."

"Started on what?" David asks.

L. Frank Baum looks from David to me and smiles. "A secret project. Right, Meggie?"

"Right," I say.

Mr. Baum walks to the door, then turns back to me and makes a long, low, exaggerated bow, the kind you might see people doing on a stage. When he comes up again, his words somehow sound like they come from a play as well.

"O brave new world, that has such people in 't."

Have I heard that before? I'm pretty sure I have.

"That's a quote I picked up in one of my dreams," he explains.

Then he's gone, and David and I stand there for the longest time just staring at the door.

Finally, David turns to me and says, "Girl, L. Frank Baum thinks you're awesome."

· 34 ·

Mom gets home shortly after five, and I'm right in the middle of telling her about L. Frank Baum when Gil and Jennifer come in.

"Do finish telling me later," Mom says to me. Then she turns anxiously to Gil. "How did it go?"

A slow smile spreads over Gil's face. "Good."

"And you got the room number?"

"Yes, it was easy."

Relief is written all over Mom's features. "Tell us what happened."

"Well, I was able to talk to Lewis this time, and he was glad to hear from me. Said he missed his old friends in Fashion City. Again, I pretended I was working on a TV special. He was impressed with that and agreed to help. So I said I'd get back in touch with more details. Then I cut to the chase.

"Lucky for me, I remembered Lewis always loved a good joke better than anything. So I told him that a man from my building was there for Vacation 65.

"I said, 'This old guy is quite a character, and he told me the best joke I ever heard. He had me and the kids rolling on the floor. You should look him up and get him to tell it to you.'

"So Lewis got Gramps's name, and I said, 'Tell the old man you want to hear that joke called Make Room for the Carriage!'"

"Cool!" I squeal. "Gramps will know it's a message from us."

"Yeah, Lewis even repeated it back to me. 'Make Room for the Carriage!' And guess what else? He just happened to have on him a roster of current residents! I guess it's necessary in his job. And he said to me, 'Yeah, here he is. Sam Lane. Room 204.' I didn't even have to ask."

Mom is so pleased with Gil, she throws her arms around him and kisses his cheek.

"So, we can leave now, right?" I say, then turn to Gil. "Where's Colin?"

"Don't worry, Meggie B., we won't forget Colin," Gil says with a chuckle.

I feel my face go hot. Does everybody know?

"Just give me time," Mom says, "to take this new information and work out the coordinates for the Carriage. Then we're out of here."

I follow Mom to the Carriage and watch as she figures the coordinates for Farlands, and then for the Western Province. Yeah, that's exactly the way I would do it. I'm so pleased with myself, I almost tell her what I've been up to, but I decide that can wait until there's not so much going on.

"I guess we're ready to go," Mom says, and gives me a hug. "Can you believe it?"

At that moment we hear a loud noise from the living room and a booming voice.

"Police!"

Mom and I clutch each other. Is it the military police looking for Colin, or the regular police here to arrest us? We make ourselves tiny and slip out the bedroom door so that we don't reveal the Carriage. We find four military police officers in the living room. Gil, Jennifer, and David seem petrified.

"And he told you he was going to keep switching trains and buses?" one of the officers is saying to Jennifer in a very gruff voice.

Jennifer nods, apparently too scared to speak.

"Well, he's done a good job of it," the same officer says. "This is the second day, and nobody can find him."

"Well, I'm sure that's where he is," Jennifer manages to say. Her voice trembles.

"Can you describe what he's wearing?" A second officer speaks up.

Jennifer and Gil look at each other and slowly shake their heads.

"No, sorry," Jennifer says. "I didn't pay any attention."

"Okay," MP #1 says in a less harsh voice. "Not to worry. He's going to run out of food and water and money. He'll be easy enough to apprehend then."

Gil finds his voice at last. "Can you believe these kids today?"

"Ain't it the truth?" MP #1 agrees, almost friendly now.

"We just need to search your apartment," MP #2 says.

"I'd tell you if he was there," Gil says.

"But we have to search, just so we can say we did it. A mere formality, you know?"

"Absolutely," Gil says. "Let's go."

Gil and Jennifer leave our apartment with the officers. Mom, David, and I breathe a sigh of relief. If they should decide to search here . . . Well, I can't think about that.

"How did they know to come here?" Mom asks David.

"Tom," David says. "The spy."

"Well, all we have to do now is wait for the police to finish up," Mom says. "We can fly as soon as they leave the building."

"What about Colin?" I ask.

"Not to worry," Mom says. "He's close by."

"How close?"

Mom just smiles and turns on the TV. We sit in silence while a sitcom plays out. I have no idea what it's about, but I'm sure we're not missing anything. In a little while Mom gets up and nukes enough frozen dinners for everybody. Then she sits back down and we wait some more. At seven-thirty the Gilmores still haven't come back. We try to eat our food, but most of it goes into the garbage disposal. Then Mom begins to pace. David and I go out on the balcony to see if we can hear anything from upstairs. Nothing.

Ten past eight. I'm frantic. After lockdown, Jennifer and Gil can come through the trapdoor, but what about Colin? Wherever he is, he'll be locked out.

Eight-fifteen. I can't be still. "Where is he, Mom? Do you know?"

"Yes, and I'm going for him right now," Mom says with sudden resolve. "It's a huge risk with police in the building, but I have no choice."

"You have only fifteen minutes!" David tells her.

Mom opens the front door and peeps into the hallway. "All clear," she says. "You two stand right here and hold the door ajar until I return."

She leaves, and David and I stand silently waiting for her return. I can hear David's ragged breath, and my heart is thundering. Hurry, Mom, hurry.

In only a matter of seconds Mom is back again, and Colin is by her side.

"Nobody in sight," she says as they come in.

Mom closes the door and locks it.

"Go to David's bathroom," she says to Colin. "And stay there until we call you."

He nods and obeys.

"Was he at Bonnie's?" I ask Mom.

"Yes. Gil and I asked her before work yesterday morning if Colin could hide in her apartment for the day. We didn't know then that it would be two days."

"Weren't you afraid she would vacillate and spill the beans?" I ask.

"We were a bit nervous," Mom admits, "but we reasoned that she had three brothers killed in the wars. So we told her we had a plan to save Colin and all of our children from the military. We told her we had found a way to leave here, and that she could come with us if she wished."

"And what did she say to that?"

"She said no," Mom says. "So we gave her the book and she was very excited. She said she could do more good by staying here and joining the Resistance, as Gil's wife did. It's almost like she's been waiting for somebody to tell her what to do. Now she seems filled with resolve and new purpose."

"Wasn't she curious about how we're getting away?" I ask.

"Yes, she was, and Gil told her we're leaving in a glass rocket," Mom says.

"What did she say?"

"She just chuckled and said, 'Okay, don't tell me, then.'"

I'm glad that telling the incredible truth worked better for Mom and Gil than it did for Gramps in the barbershop.

"It's time for curfew," Mom whispers to me and David, and I can see that she's nervous. "I hope all is well upstairs."

In a few moments Tom is at our door counting heads.

"The police have been at the Gilmores' apartment all evening," he tells us in his gossipy voice.

"Are they still there?" Mom asks.

"No, they just left, but I think . . ."

Tom doesn't finish his sentence. It seems that something has just occurred to him. He gives each one of us a funny look, then actually pokes his bony head inside the door of our apartment and looks around.

"You think what?" Mom says coldly to him.

"Maybe I should call them to come back and search here," Tom says, then watches Mom's face closely.

"Why don't you do that?" Mom snaps at him.

Tom abruptly slams and locks the door. We fall against it.

"Do you think he'll do it?" David says.

"I don't know," Mom says, "but we've got to get out of here ASAP."

· 35 ·

The Family Hour has just come on when Jennifer and Gil sneak in through the glass doors.

"Please tell me Colin's here," Gil says.

"Of course he is," Mom replies. "Now we've got to hurry."

The six of us gather quickly in the bedroom, where the Carriage is standing tall and as straight as an arrow before us. We get in, and Colin, Jennifer, David, and I settle on the floor along the back wall. Gil stands beside Mom. Mom quickly locks the Carriage door and lights up the control panel. Her fingers begin to move over the keyboard.

"Farlands!" she says out loud. "Vacation 65. Room 204. Here we come!"

We hear a gentle swoosh. The Carriage is in operation. It's uncanny, but at that moment I think I hear noises moving through our apartment, as if someone is coming. But the Carriage is soundproof, I tell myself. It's only my imagination playing tricks on me. Surely I'm just remembering the last time we were about to leave in the Carriage. I guess I'll never know for sure, because Mom strikes the palm of her hand against the bar that reads OPEN THE GATE.

Cries of astonishment follow as the Carriage is enveloped in a white vapor and we move swiftly through the gate and into another dimension. On the other side, we can see nothing but black space around us. Not one twinkle. But we can see each other by computer light. For a long time the only sound is the hum of the Carriage.

When the Gilmores find their voices, they speak in whispers, like they're afraid somebody's going to hear them. Then we all break into excited chatter. In the middle of the conversation—*Whoosh!*—the Carriage settles onto a level surface.

When the vapor clears, we see that we're in a place resembling a hospital room. And there's Gramps sitting on the side of a bed looking at us with a huge smile on his face! He's fully dressed and ready to go. He says something, but we can't hear him.

Mom gives one brief, clipped order to us, her passengers. "Stay where you are!" Then she flings open the door and runs to Gramps. They hug each other. "I was so scared for you," she says with a tremor in her voice.

"I was a bit scared myself," he says, then laughs way too loud and too long. When he speaks again, he slurs his words. "When that Lewis fellow said 'Make room for the

Carriage,' I knew we'd be flying tonight! And it looks like the whole gang is flying with us!" He throws up a hand to us. "Hey, y'all! As they say in North Carolina."

"Dad!" Mom says. "Are you loopy? Have they drugged you?"

"I reckon it was the cookie," he says. Then he burps, touches his mouth, and giggles.

"What cookie?"

"They forced me to eat the thing. I didn't want it."

Mom seems alarmed. "How long ago was that?"

"Oh, maybe an hour. But don't worry, it was only an appetizer." He laughs uncontrollably.

"Appetizer?" Mom says. "What do you mean?"

"The main course will be coming in that door any minute."

"What's the main course?"

"A hypodermic needle as big as my arm."

"Then let's get out of here!" Mom says, and takes Gramps by the hand.

"Okay, just one more passenger," Gramps says. Unsteadily he gets down on his knees and peeps under the bed. "Here, kitty, kitty," he calls. "Here, kitty. You can come out now."

I am bowled all the way over when I see who comes crawling out from under the bed. It *is* Kitty. My Kitty!

There's surprise all around, but no one seems more wide-eyed than Kitty herself. Still dressed in her purple shirt, she looks at the Carriage, then at me, and is unable to say a single word, which I know is a first for her.

"I collided with her out in the hallway a while ago,"

Gramps explains to Mom. "Poor little kitten was scared to death. I told her to get in here." Gramps has another giggling fit. "And . . . and I didn't have to ask twice." He wipes his eyes on his shirtsleeve. "She said they were about to stick her with a needle when she bolted."

Mom gives Kitty a quick hug and says, "You're safe now. Let's go."

The three of them are about to move toward the Carriage when the door of Gramps's room flies open. Just as Gramps predicted, a nurse holding a large hypodermic needle comes in. At the sight of us, she stops in the doorway and stares.

"What on earth?"

From behind her, another figure emerges, and pushes past the nurse.

"I smell them! I smell them!" he screams. "It's the aliens!"

All my emotions rise up in my chest. OMG. I feel I must scream in Chromish or burst. It's the man with the purple birthmark again! No matter where I go, he barges into my life. Will I never be free of him? I swallow and breathe, swallow and breathe.

A broken handcuff dangles from one of his wrists. At the sight of the Carriage, he's momentarily discombobulated. Gil leaps from the Carriage and blocks the nurse and the madman from coming any farther.

"Get in!" he yells to Mom.

From inside the Carriage, David is also yelling, "Come on, Mom!"

That's when bedlam breaks loose. The nurse begins to

scream, an alarm sounds, and two uniformed guards rush in. Once inside, they stop in their tracks and stare, obviously too confused to make a move.

The madman finds his voice again and starts yelling, "I told you so! I told you so!"

And before Gil can stop him, the man has slugged Mom right across the side of the face. She falls like a rock, and it's obvious she's out cold. Mom? Mom. No, Mom, no!

The pressure bubbles up into my throat, and the panic begins to move into my vocal cords and my mouth—my tongue! I am about to explode into a fit. But I don't. Instead I listen to a new but somehow familiar voice that comes from deep inside me.

"Calm, Meggie, calm. Remember you are true blue now. And at a moment like this, nobody needs a hysterical kid."

It's my own voice. It's the bigger me.

Yes, now is the time for a cool head, and action!

Everything happens at once. Gil punches the madman with all his might and sends him reeling into the wall. He lands on his face and stays there. The nurse and the guards back away from Gil, and Colin, David, Jennifer, and I tumble all over each other trying to help Mom.

We fall out the doorway of the Carriage, then half carry, half drag her to safety. Gramps is stumbling around trying to help, but he can't get out of his own way. When we get Mom to the Carriage entrance, Jennifer and I crawl inside, then tug Mom in while Colin and David push. She's still unconscious, and lies like a lump of clay in the middle of the Carriage floor.

Oh, Mom, please move. Please open your eyes. Please be okay.

In the meantime Gil continues standing his ground, preventing anybody from getting close to the Carriage. And surprisingly, nobody makes a move toward us. The nurse has dropped the needle on the floor, and the guards are bug-eyed with amazement. It's like they're watching a suspenseful movie and can't wait to see what happens next.

Kitty's eyes are darting from one person to another. I gesture for her to come into the Carriage, and she leaps at the chance. Gramps stumbles in behind her, followed by David. The madman begins to move.

"Come on, Dad!" Colin yells. "Everybody's in!"

Colin climbs aboard, and Gil backs slowly toward the Carriage door, keeping an eye on the people in the room.

The madman scrambles to his feet and begins hopping around like a Mexican jumping bean. "I told you so! I told you so!" he cries over and over again.

Suddenly one of the security guards finds the presence of mind to take a swing at Gil, but his efforts are no match for the adrenaline pumping through Gil's veins at the moment. He dodges the blow, forcefully pushes the guard away, and then falls through the Carriage doorway. Gramps, who is closest to the door, somehow finds the wherewithal to pull it shut and fasten it securely.

I look around. Are we all here? Did everybody get inside? Yes! We're in a pile, but we're all here. The people outside still are doing nothing, except for the madman, who continues to rant.

Gil is holding Mom's head. She opens her eyes briefly. A huge lump is rising on the side of her face. Has that awful man broken my mom's pretty face?

"We're safe, Mom," I whisper to her before she closes her eyes again.

"Is she okay?" Kitty says in a tiny voice.

"She'll be fine—in a little while," Gil says.

And how long is a little while? Nobody knows, but all eyes go to Gramps. He's lying against the wall, humming, with a silly grin on his face. Even without the Carriage, he has gone into space.

"He's too drunk to drive," David says.

"What now?" Colin asks.

More people have come into the room. They surround the Carriage and stare at us through the transparent walls.

"She'll be woozy when she wakes up," Gil says, "but she'll be able to fly. We'll help her."

"Who're you kidding?" Colin says, seeming disgusted. "We can't wait for her."

I think at this moment I would enjoy punching his lights out.

The madman is now pounding on the side of the Carriage, and the other people ignore him. They act like we're the freak show instead of him.

"Why hasn't somebody put him back in handcuffs?" I say angrily. "Or at least muzzled him?"

But nobody seems to notice that I have spoken.

"Colin's right," David says. "We can't wait for Mom. I

don't think the Carriage will keep us safe forever. We really need to get out of here."

I crawl out from under all the legs and go to the control panel.

"I know how to search for the coordinates," I say.

"The whats?" somebody says.

"The coordinates. It's a set of numbers."

I look up and see the purple birthmark about a foot from my face.

He can't hurt you, Meggie, I tell myself. Ignore him.

"You don't know how to fly this thing," Colin says, and I find he's standing right beside me.

I don't answer him. I have to concentrate. I search for the first number.

"Meggie." David speaks up from somewhere. "Do you know what you're doing?"

"Yes, I do. Now, don't interrupt me."

I find the first two numbers.

The madman is screaming right in my face. I can hear a muffled roar, but I can't make out his words, thank goodness. There must be at least a hundred people in that small room by now, and all eyes, inside and outside the Carriage, are focused on—guess who? Me.

With fierce concentration I punch in the third number.

"David," I hear Colin say. "Don't you think you should stop her?"

"No," David answers. "If she says she can do it, she can."

Thank you, David, thank you.

I find the fourth and fifth numbers and enter them.

Three more numbers. The Western Province. Ask for a secluded landing site. Hit the bar. OPEN THE GATE.

The Carriage moves smoothly through the gate and takes us into another dimension.

"I think you did it, Meggie!" David cries excitedly.

Yes, we're through the first hurdle. I can only hope that my calculations for the Western Province are right.

"I wish I could have seen their faces when we disappeared," Jennifer says with a nervous giggle.

"How do you know we're going in the right direction?" Colin asks me.

"I *don't* know for sure," I say hotly, "but you know what, Colin, I did my best."

It finally occurs to me that David was right about Colin. He's way too old for me.

I sit down beside Kitty and find that she's trembling.

"Don't worry," I whisper, and put an arm across her shoulder. "We're safe."

"I'm not worried a bit," she says to me. "I'm just so excited I'm about to bust!"

"You're not scared?" I ask her.

"Scared?" she says. "Did you see the needle that nurse was holding? Now, *that's* scary! She was gonna use it on Gramps. They had one for me too, till Gramps snuck me in to hide under his bed. Said for me not to worry, that Meggie B. was coming for us both. Then I knew I was saved."

· 36 ·

Mom groans and tries to sit up for the third time, but once again Gil makes her lie still.

"Take it easy," he tells her. "You're safe."

Enough time has passed that we've settled comfortably on the floor. Kitty and I, Jennifer and David, and Mom and Gil are in pairs. Colin is slouched under the control panel, while Gramps is still beside the door, sleeping it off against the wall. Kitty has peppered me with a million questions.

"What happened?" Mom whispers, and touches her cheek. "I feel like I've fallen off the Empire State Building."

"The what?" says Gil.

"Never mind. Where are the kids?"

"Everybody's here and safe," Gil says.

She sits up, and this time Gil doesn't stop her. "Where are we?"

"Meggie figured the coordinates, Mom," David says. "We're on our way to the Western Province."

Mom looks at me. "Meggie?"

"Yeah, Mom. Now, don't get mad, but I studied the tutorial."

"You used the Carriage computer!" she cries. "Without supervision?"

"Yeah, Mom. I know I wasn't supposed to, but I was bored, and . . . well, I did learn."

Solemnly she studies my face for a long time. Then her face relaxes into a smile. "That's my Meggie. I always knew if things got too tough on the ground, you'd learn to fly."

Sounds to me like a good slogan for life.

My eyes meet David's, and I find that he's smiling at me too. It hits me then that I've finally learned to do something my brother can't do. And the best part? He actually seems proud of me.

Gramps stirs, groans, and says, "Are we there yet?"

"But how did you do that, Meggie?" Mom asks me. "The tutorial's in Chromish. I know you can speak it, but you never learned to read it."

"I think Dad taught me."

"How is that possible? You were only three when he died."

"I know," I say, "but I remember certain things."

In a little while Mom is able to stand, and everybody makes way for her to go to the control panel. I show her how I figured the coordinates, and she hugs me.

"I think you nailed it, sweetie," she says.

"How do you feel, Mom?" David asks.

"Surprisingly good," she answers. "I can speak okay, and I can move my jaw around without much pain."

"But you had a pretty hard blow," Gil says. "We're going to get you to a doctor as soon as possible."

"I sure hope they have good doctors in this place we're going," David says.

"Did you know," Gramps says, sounding almost like himself again, "that the Carriage is designed to move in and out of dimensions in the blink of an eye? It's also able to find secret gateways, hidden passageways, and holes in space, so that it can travel more efficiently than any other vehicle in the universe."

"That's right," Mom adds, "and I don't know how long we'll be traveling this time, so what we need to do is record our memories in the Log, while they're fresh."

She instructs David to find the Log in the storage compartment. He hands it to Mom, and she passes it to Gramps. "You'll have to do the honors," she tells him, and touches her cheek. "I don't think I can handle it today."

"Play some scenes from our Earth first, Gramps," I suggest. "So Kitty can see what the Log does. She's the only one who hasn't heard it yet."

As the images flow out and the mystic music, so like a pan flute, wafts around us, Kitty's face breaks into a huge grin.

"Wow!" is all she can say. "Wow!"

When we begin to record memories from Fashion

City, I'm not surprised that our friends have few good ones to save. Of course, the Gilmores lovingly store memories of the wife and mother who was taken from them. Then they move on to the singing nights, before and after the Blues came into their lives. They also save some touching moments from the years when Jennifer and Colin were little and they were as happy as a family could be under the circumstances.

Kitty wants to recall her grandmother, who died when she was small, and she wants to save memories of her mom teaching her to sew, and her dad reading with her. I start to remind her once again of a guy named Corey Marshall but think better of it. Maybe, if she wants to, she'll tell me about him later. After all, it was a secret between me and the other Kitty.

When everybody's finished recording, Kitty asks, "Now, where we goin' to?"

"You mean to say, 'Where are we going?'" Mom automatically corrects her. "You don't need to add the preposition *to*. It's not necessary."

"Ohhh-kaaay." Kitty lets that word come out low and slow, as she rolls her eyes at me.

"Don't mind Mom," I tell her. "She can't help herself."

"Oh, Kitty! I'm sorry," Mom says. "I should never correct your manner of speaking. It's so uniquely you."

"Lady, are you calling me grossly unique?" Kitty says, pretending to be offended.

"Yes, I am," Mom shoots back. "And as Meggie will tell you, it's a compliment! In fact, each one of us is an original, Kitty. We should celebrate our differences instead of discouraging them."

"I'll second that!" Gramps agrees heartily. "And now we have to deprogram each other from all that brainwashing in Fashion City."

He's being polite. What he means to say is that the *Gilmores* need deprogramming. They have come out of their fog, but it will take some time to remove all the conditioning from their heads.

"What's brainwashing?" Jennifer wants to know.

"It's what they did to us," Gil explains, "to keep us in line."

"That's right," Mom adds. "If you hear something repeated often enough, you start believing it, even if it doesn't make sense. And if you happen to be taking a tranquilizer like Lotus, your mind will more easily succumb to suggestion."

"Why so many wars?" Colin asks. "Surely they were not all justified."

"Fortunes are made from wars," Mom says. "And I'm quite sure the Fathers are also trying to expand their territory."

"But people gave their lives!" Colin protests.

"Not the Fathers," Mom says solemnly. "And not their children."

We're quiet for a moment as we absorb the enormity and injustice of it all.

"What about the drabness?" I speak up after a while. "Why didn't they want bright colors?"

"Color can be stimulating," Gramps the artiste

explains. "It can send the human imagination spinning into daydreams and fits of creativity. Good music inspires us in the same way."

"And so does a good education," Mom adds.

"And time?" I ask. "Why did we have no weeks or months or names of days? Only seasons."

"The Fathers didn't want us measuring time," Gramps says. "They encouraged us to live only for the moment—for that's all we had—to forget we were destined to be soldiers at sixteen, factory drones every day thereafter, and corpses at sixty-five. For the same reason, they wanted us always in a stupor. And the jobs were so monotonous that people learned to perform them even when they were spaced out."

"We should now observe a moment of silence," Mom says soberly, "for all those poor souls who are not as lucky as we are and have no means of escaping the Land of the Fathers."

When the moment passes, Kitty says to me a bit sadly, "Did you know it was my grandpa who turned me in?"

"Yeah, we heard that on *The Family Hour*," I say. "But you know what, Kitty? You can borrow my grandpa now."

She smiles. "Yeah, he already told me to call him Gramps."

"Everybody does," I say.

"So we're really going to the Western Province?" Kitty asks Mom.

"Yes!" Mom replies. "And I promise you they don't eat rats. But that's a good example of Fashion City propaganda. We believe the Western Province is a good place, and we hope to settle down there in a home of our own. Do you want to live with us, Kitty?"

"Yeah, I'd like that," she says, almost in a whisper.

"Now that everybody here knows the truth about the Blues," Mom says, "I have to ask you to keep our secret, at least until we learn more about the people in the Western Province."

"Of course," Gil agrees. "The kids and I have discussed it already."

"I won't tell," Kitty says. "Who would believe me?"

"Well, that's the last time I'll go on vacation," Gramps says. "When I left, the plan was to go to a planet called Tranquility."

"It's a long story, Gramps," David tells him. "And we'll tell it to you later."

"What can we do to help the people in Fashion City?" Kitty asks.

"When we're settled," Mom says, "we'll help the Resistance through their contacts in the Western Province."

"Can't we use this flying thing to get some of them out of there?" Kitty asks.

"Good idea," David says, "and I bet you'd fly out your cousin Emma first."

"You know her?" Kitty says.

"I met your uncle Ethan," David says. "I'll tell you all about it sometime."

"Yeah, I would definitely save Emma and her whole family," Kitty says.

"I'd rescue Elvis" comes from Gramps.

"Bonnie," from Colin. "She saved my hide."

"Lewis Jones," Gil says, "among other friends and relatives."

"A kid named Jeremy," David says.

"I'd save Alison Fink and L. Frank Baum," I say, "and their families too, of course."

At that moment we come to a sudden but smooth landing. When the vapor clears, we look out upon the land. We are on a hillside overlooking a valley. Down there we can see a small village—a school, a church steeple, rows of houses and barns, cars in driveways, dogs playing on a green lawn, and blue hills in the distance.

It looks like home.

ABOUT THE AUTHOR

Ruth White, author of the Newbery Honor Book *Belle Prater's Boy*, has written eleven books, most of them set in the Virginia mountains, where she grew up. In high school she watched television shows that took her far away from home, fueling her imagination. Ruth was fascinated with anything mysterious and eerie, such as *The Twilight Zone*, *The Outer Limits*, and *Star Trek*.

Ruth says: "One thing I liked about *The Twilight Zone* was its trick of misleading the viewer into thinking something was a certain way; then you found out through a sudden twist that things were totally different from what you were led to believe. I wanted to use that kind of twist in a story of my own, with young adults as the main characters in an oppressive society where it was a crime to be unique—a place where people were brainwashed through the media. This book is unlike anything else I've written."

While Ruth White's story takes place in another world, she happily resides on our planet, in Hummelstown, Pennsylvania.